SECRETS OF THE SCROLLS

Mereo Books

2nd Floor, 6-8 Dyer Street, Cirencester, Gloucestershire, GL7 2PF

See more about Mereo Books at
www.mereobooks.com, www.mereo-books.com and www.memoirsbooks.co.uk

Secrets of the Scrolls

ISBN: 978-1-9191788-3-7

First published in Great Britain in 2026
by Mereo Books,
Copyright ©2026

Typeset in 11/16pt Garamond
by Ray Lipscombe Design.
Printed and bound in Great Britain
Mereo Books is trade marked

See more about John Treweek at www.johntreweekbooks.com

John Treweek began his working life as a medical researcher at University College London. He soon realised that scientific research was incompatible with his ambitions to write, and returned to academia to complete an MA in Cultural Studies, with the intention of teaching the subject.

In the early part of this new career, he founded and ran a professional theatre company whose productions were reviewed in The Guardian. He later stepped away from theatre and, after retiring as a college director, turned his full attention to long-form fiction.

He is currently completing the five novels he had long planned to write but never found time for. These novels, listed below, are scheduled for publication at yearly intervals. His website is www.johntreweekbooks.com.

The Parramatta Packet

A female Australian historian is asked to prepare a newly discovered journal written by a female convict on the First Fleet, and finds herself drawn into a hidden personal history that reshapes her understanding of the past.

Looking for Jeasop

Thomas Jeasop, a neuroscientist with a radical theory of mind, finds himself unable to publish his ideas and is instead driven to examine his own life, memory and identity through a series of dreams and reflections.

The Big Snow Dossier

An astronomer who has discovered a method for detecting catastrophic asteroids quietly prepares his family for the end of the world, raising unsettling questions about knowledge, responsibility and survival.

Cat's Turn

Dick Whittington's cat tells his own version of their shared life, offering a sharp, playful and unexpected retelling of a familiar story.

JOHN TREWEEK

SECRETS *of the* SCROLLS

As a young archaeologist investigates the secrets of an
ancient Roman villa buried by the eruption of Vesuvius,
she begins to learn more about herself.

CHAPTER 1

The Photograph

Both Jeannie's arrival at the excavation in the Bay of Naples and her response to the cache of scrolls found there can be traced back to a disclosure by her mother. She came home from school to find her in the kitchen, looking serious and trying not to show it.

'What is it, Mum?' she asked.

'I've been clearing your grandfather's house,' her mother said with a forced smile, 'and I found this parcel in an old tin chest in the attic.'

Jeannie looked at the brown paper parcel on the kitchen table as her mother began to unfold it, her eyes lighting up when she saw its contents. 'They're beautiful!' Jeannie said, removing the finely sewn moccasins and mittens. She looked at them closely, then held them against her cheeks and remarked on how soft they felt.

Then she wanted to know where they'd come from.

Her mother was hesitant, muttering something about phoning Jeannie's father at work and him being too busy, but saying he would talk to her later. Then she pointed out the scribbled note and the photograph tucked into the folds of the coarse brown paper. Jeannie looked first at the note. It was roughly creased, as if it had once been screwed up, and only told her: 'Archie wanted both lads sent home when he died.'

The photograph, a rare silver salt print on paper, showed what would then have been called a 'squaw' standing by a plaid blanket on which moccasins, mittens and other Native North American handicraft had been arranged. The squaw held the gaze of the camera, her right hand held out to gently indicate that it was her work spread out before us. In the way she stood, and in her looks, Jeannie saw herself – just as her mother must have a few hours earlier.

Holding the photograph, inspecting it closely, Jeannie was sure the woman pictured was her maternal ancestor, and she immediately had a clutch of questions: who is the woman, and when was the photograph taken? Was she the mother of the two boys mentioned in the note? Was Archie their father – and who was he?

To all these questions her mother answered that she didn't know. And to what seemed to Jeannie the most important question of all – what happened to the woman? – her mother, of course, didn't know that either. She only remembered one of Jeannie's father's uncles, Jeannie's Great-Uncle James, saying something about someone in the family, a long while before, going to Canada and his two sons being sent back home when he died.

When Jeannie's father came home he had little to add to this and seemed to want to play the whole thing down, reluctant to acknowledge the close resemblance between his daughter and the

Native North American woman. And at the weekend Cameron, the oldest of Jeannie's three brothers, made a surprise visit that turned out to have a purpose. Since he'd qualified as a doctor, and especially since he'd become a consultant in the town's own general hospital, Cameron had behaved as if he were the head of the family. Inspecting the contents of the package, he light-heartedly announced what sounded like the official line to be taken.

'This is very fine handiwork,' he said, holding up a moccasin. 'I wish my registrar could suture like this.' Looking at the creased note, but not touching it, he added quietly: 'Archie is almost certainly something like a great-great-grandfather and one of his sons one great-grandfather less.' Then, returning to the photograph, he remarked: 'This might well be where you get your looks from, Jeannie.'

So, without acknowledging Archie – or the woman photographed – as 'my' or 'our' ancestors, Cameron seemed to think that was where the matter ended. But Jeannie was of a different generation and had her own determination. Her school biology teacher had explained what had happened in the language of genetics, telling her that the previously unexpressed genes of the Native North American woman had made their appearance in her features. In contrast, the behaviour of her family suggested that the term 'throwback' more accurately described the situation, in that this word spoke of embarrassment: a thing that has been thought of as tawdry and something that has been forgotten, until the moccasins, mittens, note and photograph turned up to describe the source of Jeannie's looks.

The possibility – and to Jeannie the certainty – that her

maternal ancestor was the 'squaw' in the photograph was, and remained, of exotic interest. It explained the distinct feeling she'd always had of being different. And when, only a few weeks after her mother's disclosure, the opportunity arose to make her ancestry the subject of a social history project at school, she jumped at it.

She was allowed to keep the coarse brown paper package in her bedroom, but her mother and father's discomfort at the sight of it made it clear they did not want it shown around. So Jeannie photographed each item on her mobile phone. She explained the proposed project to her history teacher. She added that it would be best if it was about Scottish settlers in Canada in general, not about her family in particular. But she also mentioned that she'd liked to trace her ancestry back to Archie and find out about inter-racial mixing.

The proposal was well received by her history teacher and tutor, Will Hammond. He told her he was researching his own family history as far back as the early Victorian era. From that point on, Mr Hammond took a particular interest in Jeannie.

Jeannie was able to trace her family tree back to Archie, his parents and his siblings. On the way she discovered it was the younger of his two sons who had survived childhood, the other dying within a year of coming back to Scotland. After that, much of what she was able to find out was circumstantial. Archie's departure for Canada had not coincided with the rush to the Klondike and was not associated with any other large exodus of people from Scotland – so it was perhaps for more personal or family reasons that he went there.

Will Hammond, equipped with a book about Native North

American people, sat down with her in class to talk about the possibilities.

'You know that Archie was the youngest of six children,' he began, 'and it was likely that the family farm, to be kept as a single unit, would have been inherited by the eldest brother and might also have provided a living for the second. The information you've gathered suggests the daughters left the farm in their early twenties when they married and were no longer dependent on their parents. This would have left Archie in his early teens.'

He then considered whether the family might have been able to afford to have Archie apprenticed or enter a profession. He thought this unlikely. 'If Archie had gone to Canada with the skills of a craft, trade or profession, it's almost certain that he would have made a good living and unlikely that he'd have taken a native American for a wife and got by through trading her handicrafts as the photograph suggests.' Here he paused and asked if she was all right about going on. She replied calmly, in a way that impressed him. 'I have no delusions about what must have happened, the note and photograph say it all,' she said.

Then he outlined what he thought most likely: 'Archie may have been given the money to go to Canada, and enough to get him started. Or he might have gone there as indentured labour, in effect sold, though this was more common with orphans, or young people released from penal institutions. Whatever, at a guess, I'd say, it doesn't look like Archie was too successful. Perhaps he made a meagre living by selling the kind of craft products seen in the photograph – as souvenirs of another culture.'

Here he paused again, looking serious, and Jeannie thought he was about to tell her what he thought might have happened to her great-great-grandmother. Instead he began talking about his research into his own family history. He explained that in the early Victorian period of rapid industrialisation and empire, in families of limited means, it was not unusual to find that the youngest son, or sons, were vilified as a black sheep. He added that it wasn't like this in the wealthier families, where education for all the children could be afforded, and the younger sons would often go into the church, law, or medicine. But in families where there was a modest amount of property – particularly where this was held as land – but not enough to go round, the youngest were often kept at arm's length from the property by the eldest. With the benefit of hindsight, he said, the reason for this might seem obvious – sibling rivalry over inheritance – but from the point of view of the older brother, or brothers, his research suggested, the younger male siblings were quite genuinely, and conveniently, thought of as wastrels, and ways were found to remove them.

Here he looked round the class, conscious that he'd already spent too much time with just one student. But Jeannie had a question.

'Did something like that happen in your family?'

'Yes,' he said, 'it did.'

Having said this he could hardly leave the matter in the air, and it was clear that he wanted to tell her about his family. 'My great-great-grandfather was the youngest of five sons of a yeoman farmer in what is now Northamptonshire. The farm was divided between the two older brothers, the third was helped to rent a farm and buy land of his own, the fourth apprenticed to a thatcher, and the fifth, my great-great-grandfather, aged fourteen and without prospects except to work as a farm labourer, took the best mare and made his way to Sheffield where he worked in a foundry. He did well, becoming the foundry manager and having two boys and two girls, all given an education. He did not contact his older brothers until nearly forty years later, and then discovered their explanation for why he'd left in such a hurry. He was supposed to have got a girl pregnant in the nearby village, this, supposedly, being in keeping with his wayward nature. The story that has passed down our family is how, on his deathbed, with his right hand on the family bible and his grown-up children around him, he'd told them they were his only offspring. And in the minutes before he died, he explained why he thought he'd been vilified.'

Here Will Hammond again looked round the room, engaging the eyes of other students who were eager to let him know they were waiting for help with their social history projects. But Jeannie, seeing the book on his lap, asked what he thought might have happened to a Native North American woman in her ancestor's situation.

He shrugged, and without waiting for his answer Jeannie gave her own best guess.

'In looking at the photograph,' she said, 'I'd like to imagine that she accepted that the best thing for the boys was that they were sent back to Scotland. I'd like to think she was young enough to have more children, but with someone of her own kind. But I don't suppose there will ever be a way of knowing.'

As she was reaching her conclusion, she realised her teacher, wide-eyed and even startled, was looking intently at her lips. For a moment he seemed lost in thought, then, as if suddenly coming to his senses, he said: 'Yes, it's extremely unlikely that you'll ever be able to find out what happened to her.'

He handed her the book, saying she could borrow it, and adding that it might shed light on how things could have worked out for her ancestor. Then he stood up, taking the chair he'd brought with him, saying, 'Who's next?'

Half a dozen hands shot up. As he moved away, the two girls at the table in front of Jeannie turned to give her a long look. One whispered something to the other. For Jeannie this look was yet another step in the direction of feeling different from her classmates, and it put further distance between her and the girls she'd once called friends, girls who now spoke of their history teacher as 'Young Will' and did their best to flirt.

It also made Jeannie conscious that the school, the town and her home, were places she wanted to leave.

Will Hammond was careful not to show any special interest in Jeannie after that. When he saw his students at his desk to discuss what subjects they might like to take for their Higher Certificate, he was careful not to give Jeannie any more time than he'd given to the others. First he asked if she knew what degree she'd like to take.

Jeannie replied a little glibly, saying: 'Digging up the past is what interests me at the moment.'

'Do you mean that literally, as in archaeology, or is it history you have in mind?'

She said she expected to do best in science. She added that her memory for dates and that kind of detail wasn't good enough for history. Here he scanned the list of her projected grades and said, 'Yes, I can see what you mean. Have you thought about a degree in archaeology, perhaps using your biology and chemistry to specialise in forensics? You'll need to talk to the careers tutor about this, of course, but it may be possible to add a classical language like Greek or Latin. That way your scope for work in archaeology would be very wide, and you might also be able to work in forensic science, in pathology, as an alternative career, if that's what you wanted.'

He asked her to think about it, reminding her that she'd need to talk to the careers tutor and adding that he'd have a word with her himself, to check this out. In this way he spent less than five minutes with Jeannie.

CHAPTER 2

In college

Although what might be called Jeannie's 'love life' at university did not provide a reason for her going to the excavation, it played a significant part in what happened there.

She arrived at college in Glasgow with a sense of liberation, with no one she knew from school to look over her shoulder, or anyone from her hometown to remind her of it. She had the feeling that she could create herself in her own image and wanted to do this unfettered.

Which is to say: Jeannie was ripe for a good old fling.

So it was that when she took up with a boy on the same course, she made it clear from the very start that she didn't want it to get serious. She found it in herself to be lively, and she was attractive, so, of course, there were casualties. The first boy she went out with would have liked to tell her how he felt, as would the second, and a third would have liked it said that Jeannie was his regular girlfriend. But shortly before her second year at university was over, Jeannie came to her senses, realising how unpopular she'd become in some quarters. There was some obvious tension between two boys on her course, and a couple of the girls in the group often gave her distancing looks, making her wonder if she'd spoiled their chances.

At home for the long summer vacation at the end of the second year in college, she met up with her old school friends in a pub in the town centre, as she'd done the previous summer. But the second time around, she found this tedious. Her old school friends seemed not to have moved on; their talk, as before, consisted only of sharing stories from their year in college and complaining about not being able to get a summer job in the town, and Jeannie made her excuses to leave halfway through the evening. But whilst walking home she realised she wasn't much different. During her first two years in college she'd hardly been beyond the hall of residence, the archaeology department, the college library and the student pubs.

Her early return from her night out, together with her body language, told her mother that Jeannie had decided something. Without saying anything to Jeannie's father her mother switched off the television, saying, 'It's only the evening news and we've seen it twice already.'

A moment later her mother asked, 'What is it, Jeannie?'

'I'd like to go back to Glasgow and get a summer job. I'd like to fix up a bed-sit for next year, before all the other students come back.'

'What sort of job would that be?'

'Oh, in a café, or a bar. A restaurant maybe.'

'So you'll need some money to tide you over?'

Jeannie agreed that she would, and she'd need a deposit for the bed-sit. Her mother went to the bureau, asking Jeannie how big a deposit she thought she'd need. Whilst writing out the cheque, she asked where she'd stay in the meantime. Jeannie said she'd be able to stay in the hall of residence, explaining that it would be more or less empty, except for the few foreign students staying over.

Jeannie looked at the cheque. 'Mum, this is far too much.'

Her mother told her that anything she didn't spend would go towards next term's allowance. Jeannie said she would pay the money back from the job she intended to get, but her mother held up a hand, saying, 'Don't worry Jeannie, it'll all be straightened out.' She smiled, still looking serious. 'You know you'll look back on this as the best time of your life, so don't do anything silly, will you?'

Jeannie said, 'No, of course not,' and kissed her mother on the cheek. Then she left to pack her things.

After she'd left the room, her mother said, 'Well, that's a first.'

'What's that?' her father said as he turned on the television.

'Jeannie kissed me.'

'It's not too late to spoil her,' he said, in his preternaturally gruff manner.

Jeannie's mother did not know which way to take this. Having lived with this man for almost forty years, she rarely found him easy.

Back in Glasgow Jeannie gave all her attention to finding a bed-sit, having decided to stay in a small bed and breakfast hotel in Kelvingrove rather than in one of the university's halls of residence, since the B&B could be booked on a nightly basis. But finding a decent bed-sit in the Kelvingrove Park area, within easy walking distance of college, proved more difficult than she had imagined, and it was the best part of a week before she succeeded.

In contrast, she found work in only the second large city centre café she called into. So, almost three weeks into the long summer vacation, and with more than five weeks remaining, Jeannie began to get to know Glasgow as one of its newest residents. She met up with the other waitresses from the café, becoming familiar with a new set of pubs, but her main activity was to find her way about the city as a tourist and visit its many attractions, beginning with the Rennie Mackintosh School of Art. In this way she kept herself busy. It was only as she was coming to the end of these visits, in the week before her return to college, that she noticed something: that she'd avoided the part of the city which had been more familiar to her in childhood.

At first it struck her as odd that she'd done this. But with a little more thought she realised it was these childhood visits to the city with her mother that had, in fact, been the oddity. Arriving at Glasgow Central they would leave the railway station in a hurry, quickly passing by the curved wooden structure at its entrance, this possibly a café that she'd always wanted to go into. Then the hurry along Argyle Street until the turn into the long trek up Buchanan Street, passing what she thought of as 'grand Princess Square'. Always, as they rushed along Buchanan Street, she would look up wide St Vincent Street, her eye ascending its long and gentle rise, disappearing over a far wide-street horizon, suggesting the city was larger than could be imagined. Then the final turn as they entered the blind end of Sauchiehall Street and the sanctuary of the department store John Lewis.

Her mother would buy an article of clothing for everyone in the family. For Jeannie there was 'something a wee bit special' since she was company for her mother. And her mother always returned several times to the ladies' clothing department, where she'd try on clothes that were far too young for her. When her mother made the purchase of one of these items, she would whisper something to herself, something Jeannie overheard just the once: 'Yes, Duncan would have liked this.'

Jeannie knew that Duncan was her father's much younger brother, killed in a car crash, but at the age of seven she had thought no more about what this whisper might mean. It was in recalling this, in the week before her return to college, that Jeannie realised she'd never seen her mother wear any of the items she'd bought on these occasions.

On the Saturday before her return to her third year in college, Jeannie made one last visit as a tourist, this time to the attraction closest to her bed-sit: Kelvingrove's Art Gallery and Museum. She'd put off visiting this imposing Victorian edifice, and her first impression on entry was that it was the stuffy mausoleum she'd expected from the outside. On entering a gallery of paintings on the first floor, however, her breath was almost taken from her as she faced a portrait she'd known only as a print, hung with others along the main corridor of her secondary school. But here was the real thing! And enquiries at the desk at the entrance revealed that a much larger collection of Scottish Colourists was to be seen in Edinburgh's modern art gallery.

So, that was where Jeannie spent the last day of the long summer vacation.

Then, in her first week back in college, she met Alex, a final year history student who'd taken a year out to accompany his mother, a disabled artist, on a painting tour of Australia. It soon transpired that his mother had been tutored by one of the Scottish Colourists and knowing this made it seem that their meeting was meant to happen. Not only that, their relationship seemed to promise to be steady and this accorded with her wishes, because she intended her third year in college to be dedicated to hard work.

Their relationship had an added dimension in that Alex went to stay with his mother every other weekend, bringing back stories of the Colourists. In his absence Jeannie planned the pictures they would look at when they spent the next weekend together. In this way she was able to give her full attention to her studies, which she was now finding really interesting. In the first two years it had been about the basics, largely theory: identifying and mapping sites, excavation and recovery techniques and the conservation and preservation of artefacts. But her third year was much more hands-on, and she'd begun to specialise in forensics. She was looking forward to the final year when they'd spend more time at excavation sites, removing artefacts and doing all the work that followed.

So in this very positive way she found herself settled into her third year in college and the time just seemed to fly by. Over the Christmas and New Year holiday she and Alex went their separate ways, whilst at Easter, with only six weeks to go before his finals, he decided to stay on and work in college. Jeannie did the same. So began the period of intense revision before Alex's finals and Jeannie's own end of year examinations.

Then the results.

Over the next few days Alex was subdued and distant. Jeannie assumed this must be because he'd not got the degree he needed to stay on in college to do research.

He asked her what she was going to do over the long vacation. She told him she'd go home for a few days before starting a summer job in the café where she'd worked the previous summer. She did not mention that she hoped to save enough money to take a holiday with him before the long vacation was over, but before she had the chance to ask what his plans were, he told her he needed time at home to think things over.

On her first day back at work in the café, her mother contacted her on her mobile to say there was a letter for her, handwritten and marked Confidential. Jeannie asked her mother to tell her where the letter had been posted, then she asked her mother to forward it, declining the offer to open it to see if it was urgent.

Back at her bed-sit early in the evening Jeannie was surprised to find the letter waiting. But looking at the envelope more closely in the poor light of the lower hallway, she realised it couldn't be the same letter. If it was it would have said 'Please Forward' and bear the new address, and it would have taken longer to get to her. But the letter was addressed Confidential, as her mother had said, and the writing was his.

She took it up to her room to open it.

The first line explained it: 'I've written to you at home, and at your bed-sit, to make sure you get this letter.'

She read no further but put the letter face down on the small bedside table, thinking she should first take stock of how she felt about Alex. She was saying under her breath, 'It's been nice, it's been interesting and convenient, and the third year in college has been great, but I'm not in love and the only thing I have to fear is rejection.'

Jeannie then read the rest of the letter.

It was very short, and simply said: 'I'm very fond of you, of course, but if we'd spent less time together my degree would have been better. But nevertheless I'm grateful for the time we did spend together, without it I don't think I'd have been able to make my mind up about marrying my fiancée.'

There was no salutation; it was simply signed 'Alex.'

Jeannie was, of course, both outraged and astonished. Examining the letter again, with its first and only mention of a fiancée, she saw how it could not have been written to be more gratuitously hurtful. She realised she'd been treated like a doormat and that he must be extraordinarily self-centred. Moreover, his inability to take responsibility for not getting the degree he needed, and blaming her, was beyond any words she could think of.

Later, in a maudlin mood, having drunk several glasses of cheap wine bought at the nearby licensed shop, Jeannie began to think his mother was to blame. Then, and not long after, she was angry with herself for not seeing this side of him in the time they'd spent together. Later, in the early hours, emerging from a drunken sleep, she accused herself of doing the self-same thing. Was it enough to tell a boy that you didn't want things to get serious in order to drop him for another when it suited you? Hadn't keeping several boys interested been a part of her own pleasure?

Her mother rang again a few days later to ask if she'd received the letter. Jeannie said she had. 'It was from Alex, and he's dumped me.'

'Oh,' her mother said.

There was a long pause, then her mother said she thought Alex was such a nice young man – from what Jeannie had said.

'Yes,' said Jeannie.

After another pause her mother made a suggestion: 'Why don't you come home for your next few days off work at the café?'

Without knowing quite why, Jeannie accepted.

But the visit home was not a success. Her mother repeatedly asked why she thought Alex had finished with her. Jeannie did not disclose the details of the letter and her mother seemed insensitive to her irritation at being asked the same question. When she asked again, though using a slightly different tack, Jeannie lost patience with her, saying: 'Mum, why didn't you marry Dad's younger brother, Duncan?'

'Oh, well you know...'

'Was it because he didn't ask?'

'Well, he didn't. But it wouldn't have made any difference. You know he died.'

'But didn't he marry someone else before that?'

'Aye, and she married again straight after he was killed,' her mother said in swift condemnation.

'Arghh!' said Jeannie in exasperation. She left soon after.

On the train back to Glasgow she began to regret that she'd been so impatient. But for a while she rationalised that she'd only been trying to make a point her mother found difficult to understand. Not long after this, however, she realised she'd probably gone far too far and come across as just plain nasty. So before the train reached Glasgow, she rang her mother, making every effort to be agreeable. Her mother accepted her apology and then annoyed her still further by saying, 'Well, I expect you're disappointed.'

It was a comfort to have the job and the friends at the café where she worked. This kept her busy and provided a space in which to do some thinking. From this, three resolutions emerged. She would not be sleeping with another boy unless she felt she really knew him, and the relationship had a future. She would spend more time with her girlfriends, and the theme of her final year would be about getting a degree that was good enough to do research.

And this, more or less, was how things worked out in the last year of her degree – with only one setback. A boy she'd been out with in the first year showed a good deal of interest in her in the autumn term. She resisted the temptation until a family Christmas at home was on the near horizon, and then, after a few drinks, they went back to her bed-sit. The kissing and undressing were fine, but inside her he seemed to be thrusting out of malice, as if each stroke said, 'take that, take that, take that, you bitch,' and though she had been excited, the sex quickly became unpleasant and she pushed him away, saying, 'No, not like that.'

He knelt at the foot of the bed, his head down, groaning and clearly regretting what was happening. Then he stood, removed the condom and threw it down to leak its contents into the duvet. In another movement he grabbed his clothes and Jeannie thought he would leave her bed-sit undressed. But, no, he hurriedly put on his trousers, muttering unkind imprecations.

After this, Jeannie decided she would not be going go to bed with anyone until she was sure of his and her own feelings. And she wouldn't even consider going out with anyone until her degree was over. The responsibility for getting a good degree was hers, and hers alone.

When she attended the interview to which she'd been invited, Professor 'Robbie' Dinsdale told her that he had an ex-student called Angus who was responsible for dealing with the carbonised scrolls being unearthed at an excavation between Pompeii and Herculaneum, in the Bay of Naples. Professor Dinsdale said, 'You'll remember, I imagine, the way carbonised scrolls are dealt with from your third-year studies.' He then reminded Jeannie of the technique she'd studied in her fourth year, which she'd just written about in finals.

'The opportunity,' he continued, 'is to work with Angus, as his assistant. The pay is not marvellous, but they'll provide free accommodation and we'll apply for a grant for your research fees so that you can register for your doctorate. We needn't decide exactly what your doctorate will be about until next spring, so you'll have good time to settle into the work. And there are two possible areas for research. We could look at developing the methodology. It might be possible, for instance, to impregnate the carbonised scrolls with latex and unroll them. Another, and better, possibility is to develop a digital reader that will scan the scrolls without causing any damage.'

Here Professor Dinsdale must have seen reluctance written on Jeannie's face, for he quickly added that developing the methodology was only likely to be a part of the research. He qualified this by explaining that developing a faster, non-destructive way to read the scrolls was simply intended to get more quickly to the heart of the matter. 'That,' he said, with a knowing smile, 'is to get at the scroll's contents, so as to really get inside the Romano-Greek head. Is that all right with you?'

'Yes, that's fine with me,' Jeannie said, bringing the total number of words she'd spoken at this so-called interview to nine.

So, everything was decided, and in under a week – with June not yet out – Jeannie took an early flight to Naples, then a train to the town at the edge of which the excavation was sited.

And here she meets Angus.

CHAPTER 3

At the scavi

After she's tramped the hot and dusty trail from the railway station and found Angus in the site office, he tells her he's planned her 'induction' over the course of her first week there.

'I'll not introduce you to everyone at once, but by degrees,' he says. 'We'll go to the scroll workshop first.'

As he's saying this, Jeannie is eying the chiller cabinet, with its bottled water, next to the coffee-making machine in this surprisingly well-appointed transportable cabin.

'Then we'll go to the scavi,' he says, using the Italian word for excavations.

As they're leaving, Jeannie having pushed her holdall and shoulder bag under the table, Angus begins to describe the excavation, just as Professor Dinsdale did a few days earlier. 'The site is the villa of someone who must have been wealthy, an extensive scriptorium having been found. All the carbonised scrolls found so far are written in Greek. This points to the villa's occupant at the time of Vesuvius' eruption having been something of a scholar, but a name has not yet turned up.'

As they proceed round the edge of the site Jeannie is having to make an effort to listen to Angus because her attention is drawn by what she's seeing. There's a very large mound of friable earth, presumably the once-compressed ash and pumice that covered the villa to a depth of several metres, and there's the other cabin on site, to which they appear to be heading. This, she concludes, must be the scroll workshop, which looks nicely settled on a platform of earth scooped from the mound. Then there's the view over the excavation itself, its central area covered by a tall scaffold structure. And whilst she's taking all this in Angus is telling her that it's possible, and he hopes likely, that the villa will become a museum.

Then they're at the scroll workshop, and Angus is opening the door just far enough to call to the people inside, 'Jeannie's here. Back in half an hour. I'm just going to show her over the excavation.'

'Right,' he says, 'now for a quick tootle around.'

On the word 'tootle' Angus's accent is other than the one Jeannie's been hearing so far. This makes her curious. With a name like Angus, and having been at university in Glasgow, she'd assumed he was a Scot. But apart from the way he's just pronounced 'tootle' his accent has been that of the English Midlands. So, as they're nearing the main part of the excavation, but are not yet under the scaffold structure, Jeannie asks where he comes from.

'Well,' he says, 'I'm actually from Wolverhampton, where my father has a taxi business. He's from Glasgow. He married a local girl – I mean local to Wolverhampton – and stayed there.'

In this account of his background Angus's accent shifts between man of Scotland and boy of England. Jeannie finds herself at a half-way house, finding this both irritating and endearing. But she has little time to dwell on this because they're now approaching a group of young men working just outside the covered area.

Angus stops, to call to them. 'This is Jeannie,' he says.

It appears they've been told to expect her. They answer as a single body, all saying 'Hello Jeannie,' but in a slightly ragged fashion.

As they press on round the outskirts of the scaffolded area, Angus tells her she'll have the opportunity this evening to meet most of the students on site placement at the hostel where she'll also be staying. As they come round to the front of the villa, which is the only part that's been completely excavated, Angus mentions the 'two senior volunteers' working with the other group of students on site placement. He says this in a way which suggests he'd rather the pair weren't on site.

They stop in front of the villa's entrance. Angus explains what's happened to the double gates. The lower parts, covered in ash and pumice in the early stages of the eruption, would have rotted away long ago, he says. The upper parts were preserved by being carbonised by the waves of superheated gas sweeping down from Vesuvius in the second and third phase of the eruption. He adds that the upper, carbonised parts of the gates show what the whole gate would have looked like, and reproductions will be made – if it's decided to make the villa into a museum.

Then they make their way to the far side of the excavation. On the way Angus tells her that the other group of students she's about to meet are being supervised by his deputy, Giorgio. 'In my absence, Giorgio's in charge,' he adds.

When they're near the group of six or seven students, Angus calls to Giorgio, who breaks off from what he's doing. Some of the students look up and wave as this strikingly handsome man comes towards her. He's looking into the distance as he approaches and, as he moistens one lip over the other, she just knows there will be trouble.

The short meeting with Giorgio is only intended as an introduction and Angus is soon leading the way back around the scaffolded structure. As they pass the villa's entrance it's clear that Angus doesn't intend taking her into the covered area and she asks if she can be shown inside the villa.

Angus looks reluctant, but agrees: 'Well, I suppose we could go through as a short cut. But we've not got that much time today.'

Passing through the villa's entrance, they are faced with an incline of greyish earth, which they walk over. What Jeannie sees next resembles a pock-marked bomb-site, with walls of various heights protruding from the solidified ash and pumice. Towards the centre of this area they come to a part cordoned off by yellow-and-black-striped plastic tape. Angus points out a slit trench beyond the cordon. On one side of the trench is a partly visible wall of empty niches. 'That,' he tells her, 'is where the carbonised scrolls are being found.' Then he leads her back to the scroll workshop to introduce her to what he calls 'your team'.

Entering the workshop, Jeannie is struck by how much it's like a Tardis. As with the site office, it seems much larger on the inside than you'd expect from the outside, and contains much more than could be expected. And it's cool, the sound of air conditioning humming in the background.

Angus announces her as 'Jeannie, who's from Scotland'. The three young women at the table in the centre of the workshop smile but do not speak, and Angus explains that they'd like to introduce themselves, to practise their English, 'Oh, and show you what they're doing'.

The three smile again as Angus says he'll leave them to it.

'I'll be back at four, to see how you've got on,' he says as he leaves.

The first thing Jeannie notices, even before she's properly taken in the three eager faces, is a bottle of what looks like chilled water beside various bits of equipment laid out on the unoccupied side of the table. She advances, pointing, asking if it's for her.

In unison they say, 'Si si,' and Jeannie takes up the plastic bottle, quickly screwing its top off. She apologises between gulps, saying, 'I've not had a drink since I finished my bottle on the train from Naples... and at the airport I had a pastry that was a bit too salty... and Angus wanted to show me over the excavation as soon as I arrived... Sorry, this is great.'

The three look on, smiling at her gratitude each time she speaks.

When Jeannie's finished drinking, she says, 'Please, go on'. The one sitting opposite Jeannie speaks first.

'I am Rosa, a second-year archaeology student at the university in Naples, the city where I also live. I am here on an eight-week site placement,' she says in perfect English.

Giada and Silvia say the same, though their English is nowhere near as good. Then Rosa adds, 'We would like to show you what we do here. How the scrolls are unpicked and how the first part of each is read'.

Rosa comes round the table and sits at the place intended for Jeannie, the other two remaining in their seats. Jeannie now watches Rosa, who takes the carbonised scroll that's been placed there, saying, 'This one is yours to practise the technique on. It is loosely rolled and probably a draft being worked on by the slave-scribe. But we will see'.

She places the scroll on a square of felt cloth which covers the upper surface of a shallow metal platform. Beneath the platform is a sheet of paper with an adhesive surface, projecting a couple of inches. Rosa takes a stainless-steel spatula and shows Jeannie how it's used to break away a large piece of the scroll onto the adhesive paper. On this almost white, latex-sticky surface it could easily be mistaken for a burnt potato crisp.

'See,' says Rosa, touching the large fragment of scroll with the tips of her cotton gloved finger, 'it is too big and uneven to stick down.' She reaches forward to pick up a tool from the base of the lamp at the centre of the table. This tool is exactly like one Jeannie had in a Post Office set given to her as a child. It's a small, curved block of wood with a rubber surface and a little handle set into its flat back. In Jeannie's set this tool was used to press down toy postage stamps after they'd been moistened on a porous pad. Now, in Rosa's hands, the tool is used to crush the blackened potato-crisp-like piece of carbonised scroll into many small fragments, these adhering nicely to the paper's surface. This splitting away of a fragment of the scroll, and its crushing into a mosaic of small pieces, offends every part of Jeannie's conservator instinct and she utters a little cry of alarm.

'Is OK, is OK,' Giada and Silvia tell her. 'We have to do this to find which of the scrolls are of interest to the conservation department in Naples,' says Rosa. 'There are many hundreds of carbonised scrolls from Herculaneum in the museum in Naples. Most will be untouched,' she adds to reassure Jeannie. Rosa then vacates the seat and invites Jeannie to try the technique, advising that it might be best not to break off such large pieces 'so they'll fit more easily together on the adhesive paper'.

Jeannie is at first reluctant to damage what to her is a precious exhibit, but she soon discovers the satisfaction of breaking off fragments from the scroll and pressing each into a well-fitting mosaic, each tessera marked with its own fragment of a Greek letter.

'I will leave you to it,' says Rosa, returning to her side of the table.

During the next hour or so the four work with a high degree of concentration, keeping up a sometimes-faltering conversation in English. From this Jeannie learns how the excavation is being worked by the students on site placements. The three of them in the scroll workshop, Rosa tells her, are part of a group of fourteen. The other eleven are boys from several different countries, all staying in the nearby hostel, where Jeannie has a room. The three have been rotated round all the various jobs on site but prefer this one and hope to spend the rest of their placement here in the scroll workshop.

'It is hot and dusty outside, and the boys seem to prefer that,' Rosa tells Jeannie with a smile. 'We all speak English on site. When you come to Naples, we will speak only Italian – for you to practise,' she adds, suggesting an invitation is in the offing.

With about half an hour to go to four o'clock Rosa announces that they've done enough work on the scrolls to show Jeannie the next stage of the operation. In examining each other's work, they find they've each got about twenty centimetres of black mosaic to show for their efforts, Jeannie having caught up with them by having only a loosely rolled scroll to unpick.

The three then show Jeannie the next part of the procedure. They put aside their equipment and place their scroll-mosaic-covered piece of adhesive paper under the lamp at the centre of the table. Jeannie does the same and then, in a moment of dramatic anticipation, Giada puts a form headed 'University of Naples' before each of them.

Then Silvia switches on the ultraviolet light. Immediately, the lettering on each mosaic glows.

'See!' says Rosa, conductor of this magic.

'Wow!' says Jeannie, who, though she'd recently described this use of such an ultra-violet light in her final exams, had never seen it used on site.

Now, very calmly, Rosa explains what's to be done. 'We transcribe what is written in Geek onto the space on this form,' she says. 'Then, Jeannie, you translate from Greek to English in the space bellow and you decide which of the scrolls is to go on to the conservation department to be fully unpicked and which will stay here in the cabinet behind us.'

'How do I decide which scrolls go to the conservation department?'

'You will see when you have translated!' says Rosa in triumph.

The four of them set about copying the Greek letters from their carbonised mosaics onto the form Giada has put before them.

Jeannie, in theory, should be able to do this more quickly than they can, having followed the advice her history teacher gave her and taken a Higher Certificate in Ancient Greek. But her scroll has several crossing-outs, and corrections, and she makes the mistake of thinking about its translation as she's doing the transcribing.

Having finished, she looks up to find the three of them waiting. 'You've got the hang of this, haven't you?' Jeannie says with a smile.

'Si si,' they smile back.

Giada, who's on her left, can see Jeannie's scroll and says something in Italian to Rosa. Coming round to Jeannie's side of the table Rosa explains that even before Jeannie's scroll is translated you can tell it's not one the conservation department will want to keep. Looking over Jeannie's shoulder, she says, 'Look, the crossing out confirms it is a draft being worked on. All you need write on your form is that this scroll is a draft, and it will stay here.'

Rosa then asks Jeannie to translate the scrolls the three have transcribed. Jeannie does a quick translation of the first line on Giada's form: 'Roughly, it says, There were many good stories that evening, but the best were mine'. Rosa explains that the handwriting, and what's said, mean the scroll is a finished script written by the owner of the villa, the slave-scribe's master, and will need to be sent on to the conservation department in Naples. Giada writes out the translation Jeannie has just done as Rosa invites Jeannie to look at her transcript. 'Look,' says Rosa, 'mine is set out as lines of poetry and for that reason it is one the conservation department will want sent to them. But will you translate some lines for us, please?'

Jeannie does a quick scan of the first few lines of the neatly written verse. 'It looks like part of an epic poem, and might be

Homer,' she announces, before translating a couple of lines for them. And, when she's done this, it's Sylvia who announces that this is the first time they've seen a translation of any of the classics texts they've worked on. Rosa and Sylvia say 'Si si' and nod their heads vigorously in agreement, letting Jeannie know that seeing the translations is something they feel they've missed out on.

In this way, they work through all four scrolls, deciding that three will be sent on to Naples and one – the scribe's draft – will remain here in the cabinet. And it's during this whole process that Jeannie comes to understand the reason she'd been appointed to work at the scavi.

'What happened to the scrolls before I arrived?' she asks to confirm this. It's Rosa who answers, telling Jeannie that before she arrived all the scrolls would go the conservation department. Only the drafts made by the slave-scribe would come back. On the form it would say something like 'Written by the scribe with changes made by the villa's owner'.

'So, my job is to sift these scrolls, separating the ones to be kept here and the ones to go on to Naples, because I can read Ancient Greek?'

'Yes,' Rosa says, adding, after a short pause, 'You did not know this?'

'Oh, yes I knew it – but I hadn't quite visualised the set-up,' Jeannie fibs, now fully understanding why she needed to speak only nine words at her interview with Professor Dinsdale to secure this post at the scavi – and even they were perhaps nine too many. Her immediate feeling is one of displeasure with Professor 'Robbie' Dinsdale for not being explicit about the reason for her selection. With Angus, it's a sense of irritation for his unseemly haste in setting her to work. And there's also an element of disappointment, because she thought she'd been appointed because of all the hard work she'd put into her degree. But this mixture of feelings is tempered by what might be called the nature of Jeannie's determination, for she now thinks, *Well, here I am. There's nowhere else I'd rather be, and I'll make the project my own.*

When Angus returns at four, as promised, they're all waiting, sitting by their work and chatting. Angus does his rounds, looking over each of their shoulders to read the comments written on the forms.

'Good! Good! Nothing short of brilliant!' he says when he's finished.

Rosa, Silvia and Giada look pleased to hear this and do not seem surprised when Angus tells them that as they've worked so hard today they're free to catch the early train. They quickly gather their things, saying 'See you tomorrow, Jeannie,' as they leave.

'Right,' says Angus, in a very business-like manner, 'I'll show you what's to be done with these.' He takes a large pair of scissors from the centre of the table, then takes up Rosa's mosaic, saying, 'We cut off most of the excess adhesive paper, leaving a couple of inches, then we wrap this round what's left of the scroll itself, with the scroll fragments on the inside. Then we wrap the form you've just put your comments on around this and secure it with a couple of elastic bands.' Having done this Angus takes a felt pen from his shirt pocket and marks Rosa's rolled-up package with the words: 'One of the Classics.' He watches as Jeannie copies this procedure with the scroll she's worked on and then hands her the pen, saying:

'Mark it Draft Document, would you?'

When all four scrolls have been rolled up in this way Angus shows Jeannie what's to be done next, taking her scroll to the cabinet at the back of the workshop. The open doors reveal a wall of small pigeon-holes, each sized for a single scroll. About a quarter of these niches already have a scroll in them and Angus asks Jennie to put hers in the next available hole. He then turns his attention to the other three scrolls he's left on the table, slotting them into the small aluminium case he's brought with him.

'We'll take these to the conservation department in Naples, tomorrow,' he tells her. 'Right, let's get off to the hostel. I've put your bags in my car.'

His car is beside the workshop, close to the portable toilets, which Jeannie had not previously noticed. After they've driven something like a hundred metres, Angus points out the road going directly to the hostel, the road she'll walk in the morning, saying he's going to take her by a slightly different route today so he can show her the café-restaurant where the students meet up in the evening. He points it out a few minutes later, saying, 'I don't know what we'd do without it'.

The hostel is a modern building which looks like it was quickly thrown up on an unpromising patch of dusty ground at the railway station end of town. Inside it's clean, if basic. As they go up to the first floor, Angus carrying her bags, he tells her that her room is north facing, overlooking the countryside, and shouldn't get too hot. In the room, having put her bags on the bed and handed her the keys, he tells her that each of the three floors has toilets and showers.

'Oh, yes, and each floor has a kitchenette.' Leaving, he says, 'See you tomorrow at eight.'

The speed with which Angus has brought her here, the abruptness of his leaving and the slight light-headedness caused by the lack of food provide Jeannie with a sense of unreality. It's hard to believe that so much has happened since she left Glasgow early this morning and she needs time to take this in. But first she must have something to eat, and something to drink. So, she takes a tea bag and the small carton of sterilised milk from her overnight bag. Making her way along the corridor to the kitchenette, the only sounds to be heard in the hostel are the ones she's making. Back in her room she takes a small packet of digestive biscuits from her holdall. Sitting on the bed she dips the biscuits in the tea, two at a time, then leans back on her elbow to sip the tea that's left.

She wakes to the sound of footsteps along the corridor outside her door. Then all is quiet except for a door banged on the other side of the building, then, above, the sound of what might be a shower running.

She decides to get up and unpack her things, but falls asleep again. It's nearly seven when she's next woken by someone knocking on her door. Opening it, she finds the smiling face of one of the students who'd said, 'Hallo, Jeannie' as she was shown round the scavi. He offers his hand, saying, 'I am Miguel. We meet in five minutes, to go to the café-restaurant.'

He's attentive on the way there, explaining that the café will have put several tables together for 'the dozen of us'. And Jeannie is further surprised by his vernacular English when he adds: 'It is very convivial at the café-restaurant'.

A moment later, Miguel says, 'It is a pity the three girls of Naples cannot be with us.'

'The three girls of Naples?' Jeannie asks.

'Yes,' he says, 'the three students who now work for you in the scroll workshop.'

The next morning, Jeannie arrives at the scroll workshop at about ten minutes to eight. Rosa, Silvia and Giada arrive together a few minutes after the hour, saying there was a problem with the train. They go to the plank seat they've made which overlooks the site, making room for Jeannie. They sit in silence, wishing, it seems, to resume the sleep they'd had on the train. Close on half-past eight, Angus turns up, red-faced and out of breath, saying his car has a puncture and he's had to leave it in town. Unlocking the scroll workshop, he tells Jeannie this will throw out their plans for going into Naples.

Inside, he turns on the air conditioning and stands in front of the cold air blower. 'Here, take this before I forget,' he says, handing her the key to the workshop.

The three quietly get on with their work.

'Is everything OK at the hostel?' he asks.

Jeannie says it's fine and begins to tell him about meeting the other students in the café-restaurant, but almost as soon as she starts telling him this he says he'll have to call the conservation department to say they'll be an hour or so late. He also tells her he'll need to ring the restaurant he's booked for lunch. 'It's very popular,' he says. He also mentions that he has a small hospitality budget to entertain official visitors and new members of staff. 'But only the once,' he adds.

He then tells her that as they're running late, they'll have to shorten their visit to the museum, but she'll be issued with a museum pass and be able to make her own way there in future, using the railcard that's kept in the site office.

'Right. I'm going to pick the car up, be back in about half an hour,' he says finally.

Wondering how to make best use of her time in his absence, Jeannie asks if it's OK to have a look at the part of the excavation where the scrolls are being found. Angus looks uneasy about this, glancing in the direction of her three students as if to say Jeannie should join them. But before dashing off he appears to relent, saying she'll need to find Giorgio to show her round the area under cover.

He leaves, and after she's assured her three students that she intends to spend the whole of tomorrow working with them, she goes to find Giorgio.

The first group she comes across includes last evening's host, Miguel.

'Is Giorgio working with the group on the other side of the excavation?' she enquires.

'Yes, I will take you to him,' he says with an eagerness that's more than polite. And as they reach Giorgio, and his group, Miguel says, 'I have brought Jeannie to see you, Giorgio.'

Giorgio frowns a little, his forehead creasing. 'Yes. Thank you, I will come to see your group soon,' he says. But Miguel appears somewhat reluctant to leave, until Giorgio tells him a second time that he'll come to see his group very soon.

'Angus said it would be all right for you to show me over the part of the excavation where the scrolls are being found,' Jeannie explains.

'Sure, sure,' he replies, and without a word to the group he's supervising he leads her into the area under the scaffold cover. When they reach the section cordoned off by the yellow-and-black tape, Giorgio says, 'It looks like a police investigation, no?'

'Like a crime scene,' Jeannie agrees.

'Like a crime scene, yes!' Giorgio confirms, laughing, adding that Angus is very strict about who's allowed here.

They duck under the tape and into the area where a lighting rig has been set up high above them. Giorgio switches on the lights and tells her about this part of the dig. He speaks quickly, his English strongly accented. To check that she's understood him correctly Jeannie summarises what she thinks he's told her: 'So what you've found here is a scriptorium, a kind of study-library. And as the excavation of the room proceeds you expect to find an area for reading and writing, possibly with carbonised tables, lecterns, benches and so on. The slit trench along the wall of niches is where the carbonised scrolls are being found?'

'Yes, that is how it is.'

It looks to Jeannie like they've removed a good number of scrolls, with five niches already empty, but from the size of the room – as seen from the partly excavated walls protruding from the solidified ash and pumice – it seems this must be only a fraction of the scrolls to be found.

Jeannie takes this in.

When she returns her attention to Giorgio, he speaks in a

much slower, quieter voice: 'Next to the scriptorium, where we are standing, is where we think the slave-scribe might have lived and worked. There is a hidden niche set high in the wall of his room with scrolls in it. See,' he says, pointing down.

What Giorgio has told her is slightly confusing – his describing the niche with its cache of scrolls 'set high in the wall' whilst at the same time pointing down. But having got past this slight disorientation, Jeannie has her first glimpse of a kind of magic that's unfolding. For in her mind, the thought of a slave-scribe and his cache of scrolls – and the secrets these scrolls might hold – has resonance of a special kind. It's as if a trigger she was previously unaware of has just been pressed and the thought that leaps into her mind is to wonder if what the slave-scribe has to say in his hidden scrolls might speak for all the unheard and unheard-of people: people like her great-great-grandmother, the 'squaw' about whom she can otherwise know nothing. So strong, so powerful is the feeling that comes with this thought that Jeannie has the sense that she's glowing with a special kind of radiance. And, in the next moment, she finds that her eyes are fixed on Giorgio with an intense sense of expectation.

Then, reading the danger of Giorgio misinterpreting this sudden and intense show of emotion, she quickly asks: 'Does Angus know about the niche, and the scrolls hidden in it?'

'Si, but he is not interested.'

'Do you think the scrolls are important?'

'I think they interest me,' is as far as Giorgio will take it.

'Right. Thank you for showing me this part of the excavation,' she says, already moving in the direction of the scroll workshop.

Giorgio takes a step to follow, putting out a hand as if to say, 'What did I do wrong?' before he turns back to his part of the dig.

As Jeannie emerges from the covered area she's trying to hang on to the feeling that came with the thought that the slave-scribe might speak for all the unheard and unheard-of people. But in the bright sunlight this feeling is quickly fading. And when she sees Angus's car parked by the scroll workshop, then sees him hurry from one of the portable toilets, what crosses her mind is to wonder if he's remembered to wash his hands, and with this her thoughts about the slave-scribe's scrolls are quickly lost.

Not long after, in the car on the way to Naples, Jeannie realises she has some serious reservations about Angus, and she senses that she'll need to be cautious. So when he asks her what she's made of the excavation – the part undercover where the scrolls are being found – she's careful not to say too much. She doesn't mention the scribe's room, nor its cache of scrolls set high in the wall. No, she decides, she'll leave that until later. What's best, she thinks, is to stick to technical matters. She begins by asking about the way the scrolls are organised in their niches.

'The scrolls don't appear to be organised in any particular order,' Angus tells her with a nervous driver's quick sideways glance. A moment later he adds: 'The only thing for sure, so far, is that is that the master's completed scrolls, which detail the stories he's told, and his quips, are kept side by side with the writing of the Ancient Greeks.'

Well, that must say something, Jeannie surmises – but she keeps this to herself.

In this way they have a somewhat stilted conversation that

keeps them going until they reach the outskirts of Naples. At this point Angus says he'd rather not talk, if she doesn't mind, so he can concentrate on his driving. Now able to observe her surroundings in more detail, Jeannie is struck by the thought that they could be approaching almost any city in Europe. The strip along which they're travelling has a place to have car tyres and exhausts fitted, then there's a furniture outlet, a supermarket, some medium-high residential accommodation, and the obligatory disused shell of a building that could be one of the old sugar factories she remembers seeing as she and her mother travelled up the coast of Spain, from Malaga to Nerja.

As they near the old part of Naples, Jeannie is visualising the streets she's expecting to see, with their dark volcanic rock pulsating in the summer heat. But they turn off before they reach the old part of the city, going into a road flanked by low-rise buildings of mixed heritage, and here they park outside the conservation department.

The part of the department dealing with the scrolls is a large room spanned by two long tables on which scrolls are being unpicked onto long rolls of the same adhesive paper as that used in short lengths in the scroll workshop. One such scroll, fully unrolled, together with its transcription in Ancient Greek, and translations in Italian, French and English, is at the head of the room in a long glass cabinet. This is a display for visitors.

Whilst they wait for the head conservator, who's on the phone in her fish-tank of an office, Angus takes Jeannie to this glass cabinet, explaining that the scroll was found in Herculaneum and its text is a part of the Decameron.

'It's in Ancient Greek,' he tells her, seeming to have forgotten that Jeannie will know this at a glance, 'and its translation closely resembles the ones that have come down to us through the ages. That's to say, the ones that were translated more than a thousand years ago from Ancient Greek into Arabic, then later into Latin and finally into the modern European languages.'

'And that's its importance,' says the voice of a woman coming up behind them. She is an American of slight build, with ungenerous lips, and she greets Angus very warmly, as if he's a long-lost friend. This immediately strikes Jeannie as odd, since from what Angus had said on the way here the two meet perhaps twice a week. The woman holds out her hand for Jeannie to take, saying, 'Call me simply Elaine.'

Then Simply Elaine makes a little speech:

'As my good colleague Angus was explaining, the importance of a document like this, being written in Ancient Greek and almost certainly a close copy of the original, is that it provides a check against the translations known to us. You'll remember from your history how so many of the writings of the ancient world – of the Greeks and Romans – were preserved through the Islamic conquest of much of the Mediterranean area. These ancient texts were translated into Arabic and kept in the important libraries of the Caliphate, and that's how we've come to know them, after they were subsequently translated into Latin and later into modern languages.'

Whilst Simply Elaine is saying this, Jeannie notices the way she places her hand on Angus's arm, and the way he nods approvingly at what's being said. This light touch on his arm is not at all sexual, or even affectionate, but seems more about them standing together as colleagues. In seeing this, what comes into Jeannie's mind is that it's a gesture of concealment: that this lady's not telling the whole story. Yes, Jeannie says to herself, the reading of these scrolls will be an important check on the accuracy of the known versions of the classic texts, and perhaps modern scholars will want to amend what we have in the light of these near-original copies. But there's more to it than that. It looks like Angus and Simply Elaine are colluding in something.

What then comes into Jeannie's mind – and this also explains why the slit-trench in the scriptorium looks more like grave robbery, and why Angus was so hasty in getting her started in the scroll workshop – is that the pair are in a hurry to find a particular piece of lost writing from antiquity. That is, Jeannie now suspects the pair are in a hurry to make their names by finding the equivalent of a lost Rembrandt in the attic.

As the visit to the conservation department is intended to do little more than introduce Jeannie to Simply Elaine and the other two staff who work there, they're able to get away without too much delay and make their way to the restaurant, where Angus has a reservation. Whilst walking there, to change the subject, and even sound light-hearted, Jeannie mentions that the students in the hostel refer to the students in the scroll workshop as 'the Three Girls of Naples'. Angus finds this vaguely amusing, and Jeannie takes the opportunity to mention that the three have expressed an interest in knowing more about the scrolls they've worked on. 'That is, the ones they don't see again – the ones kept by the conservation department.'

Angus is immediately defensive, stopping as they walk. 'They've been given a copy in Italian of the scroll on display in the conservation department. And they've had the translations of the opening sections of each of the scrolls returned to the workshop,' he tells her.

This over-reaction, and avoidance of saying anything further about the scrolls the conservation department retains, confirms for Jeannie that Angus and Simply Elaine are up to something.

Eating under a sunshade at the chosen restaurant at the edge of the old part of Naples is clearly a source of great delight to Angus. He introduces Jeannie to their waiter, with whom he seems very familiar, and suggests the meal he thinks she'll like, asking if she'll join him in a glass of wine – but just the one allowed by his hospitality budget. 'We'll need to be in good form for the visit to the museum,' he adds.

He explains that it's only the museum's repository they'll be visiting today, and he reminds her that she'll be able to visit the museum itself as often as she likes when her pass comes through. As he's saying this the antipasti arrives and he tucks into it like a man half-starved, taking the remaining bread left on the table. Whilst Jeannie eats, she steals glances at him now and then, knowing she'll have to try to hide her true feelings. After less than a day in his company she's got the clear impression that he thinks she's here for just one reason: to do his bidding. And she decides she mustn't leave it too long before opening up a conversation about her reasons for being at the scavi.

So, after Angus has eaten his dessert – a course Jeannie has declined – and he's comfortably sipping his coffee, she says, 'I've got until April to sort out the exact nature of my research, but I'd like to be giving it some thought from the outset.'

Angus does not surprise her when he says, 'If you've got until then, what's the hurry?' But a moment later he's giving what sounds like good advice: 'The thing to do is get your students up and running in the scroll workshop and then spend time on various jobs around the excavation. That way you'll get a variety of hands-on experience and find your own area of interest.'

This advice suggests she'll be able to mention her interest in the slave-scribe's cache of scrolls when the opportunity arises, so she decides to say nothing about them for the moment.

The collection of artefacts in the museum's repository is astonishing. There are just so many things from Pompeii that were preserved in perfect condition beneath the ash and pumice of Vesuvius' eruption. Then there are the many things made of wood from Herculaneum, carbonised within its undamaged rooms as the pyroclastic waves of searingly hot gases hit the area in the last phase of the volcano's eruption. Beds, benches, stools and children's cribs are exactly as they were made, except that they're entirely black. And from each of the two cities there's an abundance of pottery: oil lamps, jugs, cooking pots and vessels. Then there's the glassware and eating utensils, ornaments and jewellery. Also, bronze statuary, mainly of Roman gods in votive poses. Jeannie is almost overwhelmed by all this when she reaches the giddy conclusion that the finding of such objects, and the sight of the wall paintings, together with what is said in the slave-scribe's scrolls, will give her the total picture of life at the villa.

On their return Angus drops her at the scroll workshop before continuing on the dirt-track road that skirts the scavi. This, he says, is in the hope of catching Giorgio before he leaves, to see if he's found time to recover any more scrolls. Jeannie pauses before going into the workshop, reflecting on Angus's great eagerness to remove the scrolls in a way that seems to be tantamount to ravaging the site. It's clear that he's not following what she understands to be good archaeological practice: which is to say, they're not working uniformly across the whole of the villa. As she hovers by the scroll workshop door, she can't help but think that what's happening is little short of plunder.

As she enters, her three students are getting ready to leave and it looks like they feel neglected. They've managed to clear the pumice and ash from all their scrolls, and from hers. They'll be able to begin unpicking the scrolls tomorrow, and she tells them she intends to spend the whole day with them.

The next morning Angus pokes his head round the workshop door for just long enough to tell her that he and Giorgio will be spending the day removing scrolls in the scriptorium. He's cheerful, and invites her to come over to see what they're doing – if and when she's got a minute. She calls towards the closing door, 'Yes, straight after lunch.'

She is so absorbed in the painstaking task of unpicking her first tightly rolled scroll that she doesn't realise the morning is already over. 'It is time to take the lunch on the seat we have made,' Silvia tells Jeannie as she and Giada leave.

Rosa hangs back, looking over Jeannie's shoulder, saying, 'I am sorry, but I cannot invite you to stay in Naples this weekend, my mother is not well.'

Surprised by this so sudden invitation, and having plans to go to Capri this weekend, Jeannie says, 'It's very nice of you to think of inviting me, another time perhaps.'

After a sandwich lunch on the seat overlooking the scavi, Jeannie leaves her three students to see how Angus and Giorgio are getting on. A few metres into the covered area she finds how surprisingly cool it is, the white corrugated sheeting above her reflecting the worst of the afternoon heat. At the heart of the scaffold structure the lights are on, and as Jeannie approaches the taped-off area it now looks more like theatre in the round.

It seems Angus and Giorgio have been busy. The slit trench is now much deeper at one end, enabling Angus to work his way down past a series of scroll-bearing niches. He's submerged almost up to his shoulders, with barely enough room to turn around, and as Jeannie arrives he's telling Giorgio they'll have to widen the trench. They're too busy to notice her, and she's happy just to watch them working: to note how Giorgio passes Angus the tools he needs, and, in between doing this, he bags up the crumble from the trench.

It's when Giorgio has filled a bag and turned to put it on the pile behind him that he sees her. At this very moment Angus says, 'Oh fuck.'

'What is it?' Giorgio asks.

Angus stands to one side, to the extent that he's able, to reveal a hole that's appeared beneath his heel.

'Oh fuck,' he says again.

'What is it?' Jeannie asks Giorgio.

Having glanced into the trench Giorgio says, 'Is a hole, maybe where a body was. Is perhaps a body cavity Angus has stepped into.'

'Maybe. But we don't know that yet,' Angus hisses in frustration.

'But, Angus, we must stop until we know,' Giorgio insists.

'Yes, we'll stop when we know it's a body cavity. You go and get the probe camera from the site office. And don't hurry, I'm going to get these scrolls out first.'

Jeannie now becomes Angus's assistant in his haste to clear a niche of its scrolls, passing the tools Angus needs as he works to dislodge a piece of material the size and shape of an elongated skull. He has just enough time to remove this porous-looking piece of rubble before Giorgio returns with the camera. Giorgio waits for him to get out of the trench, then gets in himself, squatting over the hole made by Angus's heel. He keeps looking up to explain to Jeannie what he's doing as Angus shifts uneasily behind her, sometimes glancing over her shoulder.

'The camera is like the ones used in medicine,' Giorgio informs her, 'to look inside the body.'

'Yes,' she says, 'I'm familiar with them from my degree in Glasgow.'

Giorgio puts the probe into the hole and scans the area immediately around it. Then he goes in a little further. When he looks up, he's grinning. 'Hey, man,' he says to Angus, who's now standing anxiously above him, 'you were standing on this part – what do you call it?' he points to his own buttock.

'His arse,' says Angus, unamused.

'Si si, you were standing on his arse,' Giorgio says, chuckling to himself as he returns to his exploration. He adjusts his position several times to get the camera probe further into the body cavity.

When he looks up again, he's serious. 'It is not good,' he says to Angus. 'The man is high status, maybe the villa's owner. He is lying on his face, he has a very fine jewelled robe clasp.'

'Oh, fuck. Oh, fucking fuck,' says Angus loudly, and for a while neither Jeannie nor Giorgio speaks as the soft, pumice-dampened silence takes a hold on the whole area under cover.

When Angus eventually speaks, he manages to put both hurt and frustration into one very short sentence. 'I'll have to contact the director,' he says, and then he leaves.

When he's out of earshot, Jeannie says, 'What's going on – why is finding a body cavity such a problem?'

'If we know people were trapped here when Vesuvius erupted, we have to excavate the whole villa. You understand? To look for more bodies. This is because the villa may become a museum, and any body cavities we find, and where we find them, will be, how you say, the story of human interest?'

The thought that immediately comes to Jeannie's mind is that if the site is to be worked uniformly, end to end, then the scrolls hidden in the wall of the scribe's room will inevitably be recovered. She mentions this to Giorgio, and his answer is enthusiastic. 'Si si, I make sure it happens.'

Jeannie's next thought is one of concern, that they'll find the body cavity of the slave-scribe in his room. And it does not escape her attention that she's already wanting to know that he escaped the appalling fate of being caught up in the eruption. For a while she's preoccupied with this thought, hardly noticing Giorgio getting out of the trench and standing close to her. Until, that is, he touches her arm and she's startled into the present.

'Sorry, sorry,' he says, 'I did not want to frighten.'

'No,' she says, 'It's me – I was just lost in thought.'

She looks at him, at the intensity of his dark eyes, at the well-defined shape of his mouth, and casts a glance about her. Seeing Miguel's group of students working just outside the area under cover, at the far side of the excavation, she comes to her senses, thinking this is not a good situation to be in.

'I'll take this back to the site office,' she says, now realising she's holding the probe-camera, which he must have handed to her before getting out of the slit trench.

'I will carry it for you.'

'No,' she says. 'No, I'll carry it myself.'

Friday. Jeannie arrives early at the scroll workshop to find the door open. She gingerly approaches, thinking a break-in might be in progress, and her first glimpse inside suggests there might be, with fragments of pumice-crumble and ash spread on the table. But seeing three encrusted scrolls amongst the debris, and Angus poking about in the storage cabinet, she enters.

Turning to Jeannie, he points to the table. 'These are the three scrolls we took out yesterday, before we had to stop. They'll be the last to be removed for a while. I'd like you to get your students to do as much as possible on them today. Next week's the last of their site placement and I want them back at the dig. So could you make sure they bring suitable footwear, and remind them to bring the overalls they were issued with?'

After saying this, Angus makes his exit.

Jeannie decides she'll tell her students what's going on when she knows exactly what is happening. Trusting that they'll know what to do with the encrusted scrolls Angus has left on the table, she makes her way to the area under cover. Close by the area cordoned off by the striped tape Angus and Giorgio are in animated conversation, but it's mainly Angus who's doing the talking and the pointing. As Jeannie gets to them, he turns to her to explain that they've just pegged a line parallel to the villa's frontage, dividing the excavation into two more or less equal areas. He's to take charge of the area to the front of the villa and Giorgio, with her assistance, will take charge of the area at the rear. Angus then strides away to talk with the students gathered just within the covered area at the far side of the excavation.

Jeannie is curious about why Angus is taking charge of the front section of the villa, which excludes the scriptorium and the large number of scrolls still lodged there. She asks Giorgio about this. The tone of Giorgio's reply is amused disdain: 'Angus does not want to be near the scriptorium if he cannot take scrolls from it.'

Jeannie nods to indicate she understands this, and Giorgio seems to take this as a cue to disgorge what's on his mind, and there's much more than a hint of anger in what he whispers. 'Listen, Jeannie, I am Italian – this is my country. This is not the country of Angus who was born in England and thinks he is a Scottish man. This is not the country of the Director of Excavations. I am a graduate from the university in Milan, but not in archaeology. This means I will never be more than his assistant.'

Jeannie is as much taken aback by the suddenness of this whispered outburst as she is by its contents. Yet at the same time she's sympathetic. Angus's work does indeed look like that of the plundering outsider, and it appears that the Director of Excavations, who's also British, is a dominant if absent figure.

'So, you could never be in charge of an excavation – like Angus is at this one?'

'That is how it is,' Giorgio says.

She's sympathetic with his frustration, but finds the next thing he says almost impossible to answer.

'Listen, Jeannie, I would like to know what the scribe is saying when he writes the scrolls. You know, the scrolls hidden in the niche.' He looks around, as if concerned about being overheard, then says, 'I would like you to read these scrolls'.

Jeannie is silent. Yes, she wants to read the scrolls. She wants to know if the slave-scribe speaks for all the unheard and unheard-of people. And she already has the keen sense that these scrolls will be the subject of her research. But what is Giorgio saying?

Her silence, and her enquiring look, are taken by Giorgio as agreement. 'The scrolls are only lightly covered with ash and pumice,' he tells her, and waits for her response. When Jeannie does not answer, but only looks at him quizzically, he ventures to take his proposal a step further. 'If I borrow the scrolls, maybe you can read them. Maybe not in the scroll workshop, but in your room at the hostel?'

'Maybe,' says Jeannie, not meaning that she accepts this proposition but rather wanting to know exactly where he's going with it.

'OK, OK,' Giorgio says, quickly adding, 'I have a friend, she is a good friend, in the conservation department. You will have met her, she does – how you say? – the recording of the scrolls.'

'The inventory?' Jeannie suggests.

'Yes, that is it.'

Now, having in mind the shy woman in the conservation department who engaged her in conversation about working with Giorgio, Jeannie says, 'Yes, I met her when Angus took me into Naples.'

'That is her,' he says, and pauses before adding, 'She can be trusted.'

It's then that Jeannie understands where he's going.

'Giorgio,' she says firmly, 'if I did look at the scribe's scrolls in my own time, in my own room, they'd still have to go through the system and be recorded – you understand that, don't you?'

'Of course, of course,' he says.

Then why the subterfuge? Why mention the shy keeper of the scrolls?

It's as she's thinking this that Angus calls for them to come over. Giorgio has already turned from her when Jeannie realises why the shy keeper of the scrolls asked her about working with Giorgio, and she just blurts out, 'Is she your girlfriend?'

Giorgio stops, as if prodded in the lower back, and he turns to take a step towards her. 'Is that a problem?' he says.

'No!' she says quickly. 'Why should it be?'

He smiles and turns to walk to Angus and the gathered group of students. She hesitates, puzzled by what's just been said. Then the penny drops. She's just given Giorgio the green light. She's just told him that it doesn't matter that he's got a regular girlfriend – it won't interfere with what he intends will happen here.

She hurries to catch him to explain the misunderstanding,

but she stumbles and he's already with Angus and the students. So when she joins them, she goes to the far side of the group, intending to look composed, deciding it's best to say nothing for the moment, but she will make it clear how things stand the first time she gets the chance.

Angus stands on a chair which he's spirited from somewhere to address the students, explaining how it's been decided that the best use of their time – with only a week and a day left of their site placement – is to involve them in the excavation of the main part of the villa under cover. A cheer goes up, suggesting that this is what they always wanted.

Then he explains the plan. They'll be divided into two groups of equal size. One group will work with him on the front half of the villa where it's thought there are some interesting wall paintings to be found. The other group – Giorgio's – will excavate the rooms to the rear where a body cavity has just been discovered. The idea, he tells them, is to work their way across the villa, taking a layer of about a metre deep at a time. What they'll find in the upper layers will be largely charred roof timbers and tiles, but lower down they're likely to find many artefacts, and there may well be more body cavities. And there are the wall murals to be seen.

Jeannie is at first admiring of the way Angus outlines the work to be done and the way he enthuses the students. But when he goes on to describe how the excavated material must be sifted and sorted, she realises this is a St Crispin's Day speech, intended to rally the students for what amounts to hard labour in their remaining time at the scavi. Also, it's clear that given the size of the area under cover, this group on site-placement is unlikely to take the dig down by even a metre in the time available – and they'll come nowhere near finding either artefacts or body cavities. Added to which, revealing the wall murals will be the work of a specialist team sent here at some time in the future.

As she walks with Giorgio in front of the students allocated to him, she asks what job she's been given. Giorgio tells her that at this stage her job is to photograph each layer of the dig, with its various finds, and to supervise the sorting of all the material removed from the covered area. He adds that this was Angus's decision, not his.

By the end of the morning the system for removing the upper layer of compressed crumble, its sorting and its sifting, is well established and Jeannie makes her way wearily back to the scroll workshop. Her three students are on the plank seat, eating their sandwich lunch. Rosa tells her the work on the scrolls is going well and it looks like all three scrolls are classical texts written as lines of poetry.

Jeannie goes into the workshop to see how far they've got. Enough of the scrolls has been revealed to show that they are ones the conservation department will want to keep. Back outside, and with her three students, Jeannie explains what's going on, telling them what's expected of them next week. She says this in the full knowledge that what they'll be doing is just plain hard and dirty work. She concludes: 'I'm afraid this batch of scrolls is the last you'll have the chance to work on. Angus wants everyone on site next week, but you'll be working under the covered area and it's not too hot in there.'

She asks them to remember to bring the light overalls they

were issued with, and suitable shoes. It's obvious from their silence that they're not well pleased.

Her first Saturday in Italy is to be used to sort herself out at the hostel. She'll walk into town later in the morning and do some shopping, and this afternoon she'll do some reading on Roman history at the time of Vesuvius' eruption. But first she'll do her washing in the launderette.

She's just about to do this when Miguel comes to her room to say that he and three others will be getting together later to cook their evening meal in the mini-kitchen on the floor above. Jeannie can hardly refuse the invitation when he says all that's asked of her is for her to share the cost and help clear up. He and his friend Hermes will do the shopping, and they'll do the cooking, since there's only room for two in the little kitchen.

So it's a pleasant and productive day for Jeannie and she goes to bed thinking it's going to be hard work here, but she's optimistic that things will work out. She also thinks about Miguel. A good-looking boy, and nice to be with, but there's something about him which prevents her finding him attractive. What comes to mind is a thing a friend at college once said. This friend had turned down a boy in the year above who everyone thought was really handsome. Her given reason: simply that he wasn't her type. Jeannie had not understood this at the time, but now she thinks she does. It's as if Miguel is her younger brother, and she is someone he looks up to – or maybe it's that he makes her feel like she's his mother.

On Sunday Jeannie takes a boat across the Bay of Naples. The main holiday season is in full swing and everywhere is crowded. In

Sorrento she tries to get away from the main drag and have lunch in a restaurant recommended in her guidebook, but the restaurant is full and she has to share a table with an elderly couple from Kent. They draw her into conversation, seeming to think that because she's alone she must be lonely.

On the ferry to Capri she avoids talking to anyone who looks or sounds British, not wishing to repeat the lunchtime experience, and she finds that she's thinking of herself in a new and strange light: not yet a resident, but also not a tourist.

Reluctantly she has to take a guided tour of Capri, as this is the only way to get round the island without the considerable expense of a taxi. The tour allows one hour at the remains of what was Emperor Tiberius' palace. For most of this hour she's entranced by the amazing view from this the island's highest point. Vesuvius rises through a heat haze. It's so dominant in this landscape that it's difficult to understand why the ancient Romans did not feel threatened by its looming presence. But then she remembers what yesterday's reading of Roman history had told her; that the mountain had not erupted within the range of folk memory, and she can now see how it would have been regarded as a benign giant on whose slopes the best grapes in the Roman Empire were cultivated. In seeing the vague shape of the coastline's present towns Jeannie imagines she's looking at the scene as it would have been in ancient times when Emperor Tiberius occupied his now ruined palace. In doing this she senses that when the villa is more fully excavated she'll be able to visualise life there.

Monday. Work at the excavation is every bit as demanding as it was on Friday, but with four more days of solid hard labour before them it seems much harder. In the evening the students turn up at the café-restaurant earlier than usual. After the meal is over, they don't hang around but cheerfully say they're going back to get some rest. Some say they they've got blisters, others that they've got back-ache, though no one complains about this: rather, each regards his ache or pain as a badge of honour.

On the Wednesday Miguel does not show up for his evening meal at the café-restaurant. He's waiting by Jeannie's door in the hostel when she returns. He's red-eyed and it's clear that he's been crying. Jeannie invites him in, asking, 'What's the matter? Why didn't you come for dinner?'

'I can't talk now,' is all he says, when it's obvious that to talk is why he's here. He sits miserably on the bed.

Jeannie offers to make him tea or coffee, or would he like a drink of water? All are refused, and he tells her that what he needs is some tablets to help him through the night.

'What, to help you sleep?'

'To make me sleep forever,' he answers.

Seeing that he's being melodramatic, but not wanting to sound unsympathetic, she sits beside him, putting her arm around him, leaning forward in an attempt to make eye contact.

'Can you tell me what's happened?' she says.

'It's Giorgio,' he says, 'I won't see him again. He doesn't want me to write, and he laughed at the idea of visiting Spain. When the next group of students comes to the excavation, he will have other conquests.'

Jeannie is more surprised by what she just been told than she cares to show, and she holds onto Miguel so as not to reveal this reaction. Then, hoping she's not betrayed her surprise at Giorgio being a Lothario in both directions, and both at once, she gradually releases Miguel.

Whilst she's easing her hold, she says, 'These things happen – it's very hurtful, but feelings are often one-sided.'

Miguel surprises her again as soon as she's released him by seizing her hand, saying, 'Can I stay with you tonight?'

Jeannie gets the better of her instinct to pull away her hand, and though she knows there's absolutely no chance of letting him spend the night with her she surprises herself by wondering what it would be like if he did. After the comforting words she'd given him he'd press himself against her. She'd insist on his using a condom, of course, and for all the right reasons, but this would not protect her against the complications that would inevitably follow.

With this thought Jeannie breaks free, realising she is actually tempted by the idea of such sexual contact and must remove herself from Miguel as quickly as she can.

She chooses her words carefully.

'Miguel,' she says, 'I don't think staying the night with me would help either of us. Come on, let's get you to your room.'

Miguel is accepting and placid. She has her arm around his waist all the way up to his room. He has his key ready and goes in. She follows. He seems lost, so she asks if he's cleaned his teeth. He has not, and he does this whilst she waits. She suggests he undress but keep his pants on. He does what he asked and gets into bed.

She resists going to tuck him in, or give him a kiss, but remains where she is.

'You're feeling sorry for yourself right now, aren't you?'

'Yes.'

'Perhaps it would help if you considered whether you've done to anyone else what Giorgio has done to you.'

'Yes,' he says.

She says 'Goodnight', and steps towards the door.

'Goodnight, Jeannie,' he says before she leaves.

On her way back to her room she wonders if – as the only female member of the excavation team – such pastoral care as this will fall to her to give. If this is going to be the case, she wonders if it wouldn't be best to talk to Giorgio to head things off with future students. Then she thinks this really is none of her business. As far as Giorgio is concerned, she'll just have to look after herself.

The final week of this group's student placement ends on a high note. A small team, despatched from Naples, come to deal with the body cavity and are unpacking their things as the students arrive on site. Jeannie's job is to organise a roster so that two or three students at a time can observe the team as they do their work. She's to make sure every student is present on at least three occasions, to enable them to see each stage of the process.

This goes well, and Jeannie herself is able to witness the work in all its detail. The first thing that's done is to carefully explore the cavity with the camera probe – a camera identical to the one Giorgio had used, except that it has a CD recorder attached to it. This procedure is very much of a clinical nature: the female operative is sheathed in a body suit, her hair enclosed within something resembling a shower-cap, her mouth and nose overlaid with a mask, and she speaks into the recorder as she carefully moves the camera probe inside the body cavity. She reports that the body is on its ventral side – face down, as Giorgio had said – and the bones are all intact except for the skull which has a small dorso-lateral fracture. Stopping at this point, and releasing the recording button, she looks up at the students to tell them in flawless English that such a fracture to the skull is quite common in these victims, who were often killed by falling roof tiles or masonry. Though it could be that the fracture occurred after death, there is no way of knowing. She repeats this for each small group of students who appear at the edge of the trench above her and she does the same when removing the long bones of the leg for DNA analysis.

Jeannie is impressed by the way this woman takes her teaching role so seriously, in contrast to Angus's neglect.

When the woman turns her attention to the removal of the artefacts, with Angus and Giorgio now looking over, she informs the CD recorder that there are two large decorative robe clasps in the cavity. She looks up to say, 'The victim was a man of high status.'

After the removal of the clasps, and after they've been handed up to Angus for a closer look, he turns to Giorgio and says, 'Our man here is most likely the villa's owner.'

Satisfied, Angus returns to his part of the dig.

All the students are gathered close to the slit trench for the plaster of Paris injection into the body cavity – all, that is, except Silvia and Giada, who have not been seen since Tuesday. But there is not, in fact, much of interest to be witnessed. There are bags of plaster, a mixing machine, a long rubber tube and a man in a white overall of similar appearance to his female colleague. So, after a brief look at this final part of the procedure the students move to where the camera operator, now free of her cap and mask – and now a recognisable person – is waiting. She introduces herself as Dr Lilia and begins her talk, speaking English as if she were from that country.

'The villa, being closer to Herculaneum than to Pompeii, would have suffered some of the heaviest falls of ash and pumice, and pretty much the full force of the two main pyroclastic waves of superheated gases. The presence of the body cavity indicates that the victim died in the first of these waves of hot gases, the one at the lower temperature which only lightly cooked the people and left clothes and leather intact. The carbonising of the scrolls in the wall niches, which are several feet higher than where the man fell, would have been caused by the later, much hotter pyroclastic wave. By this time the body found here would have been entombed in layers of ash and pumice, otherwise it would have been burned to the bone by the much hotter gases.'

She stops here, inviting questions.

For a while it seems the students are shell-shocked. Jeannie is also silent – again hoping the slave-scribe escaped this dreadful fate which she can imagine all too clearly. Then questions from the students come quickly, all intrigued it seems by the thought that the early pyroclastic waves of hot gases coming down from Vesuvius only lightly cooked their victims.

It's nearly one in the afternoon by the time the body-cavity team have done their work. When they've gone, Angus asks the students to collect their things and meet him outside the site office. Here he makes another speech, this time without the advantage of a chair to stand on.

'You should consider yourselves fortunate to have been on site placement when a body cavity was discovered and to have seen its shape preserved. It's something to take back to your home universities with you.'

Here Angus pauses, inviting the cheer that doesn't quite happen.

'Now, as a special treat, and a way of saying thank you for all your hard work, I'd like to announce that your job is now done here.'

Angus pauses again. This time the students are confused about exactly what's going on, and he quickly adds: 'There's no more work this afternoon. Your hard work is finished, I've arranged for us all to have lunch together at the café-restaurant near the hostel. It's on me!'

There's a slight delay before what's meant by 'It's on me' is fully digested. When it's understood, a loud cheer goes up.

They leave the site as a single group, but soon break into twos and threes with a couple of the boys hanging back, looking like they might be sharing a spliff. Jeannie catches up with Rosa and apologises for not having had the chance to talk to her in the last few days.

'Ah, everybody has been so busy!' Rosa says.

As they walk, they make the arrangements for Jeannie's stop-over in Naples at the weekend. They've no sooner done this than Miguel comes alongside Jeannie, making clear his need for attention. Jeannie drops back to give him the chance to talk. She is uncomfortable with his so obvious neediness, but makes every effort to conceal it.

'I bet you'll be please to get home, after all the hard work,' she says, in an attempt to make their conversation matter-of-fact.

He does not respond to this, but says, 'Can I be with you in the restaurant? I have been avoiding Giorgio, and it will be difficult.'

'Giorgio's not coming. He gone to Naples,' she tells him.

'Oh, has he?' Miguel says, looking more upset by this news than he was when he thought he'd have to be in the restaurant with Giorgio. It seems he wanted to give Giorgio one last chance to be kind to him. Jeannie, having noticed how Miguel's friend Hermes so often looks admiringly in his direction, says, 'Giorgio will break a thousand hearts. It's what goes with such good looks. Have you told Hermes what's happened?

'Yes,' Miguel says, but adds nothing to this.

'How did he take it?'

'He was fine.'

'Miguel, then why not stay close to Hermes in what's left of your time here?'

On her second Saturday in Italy, after an early lunch in the rapidly emptying hostel, Jeannie takes the train to Naples. She's a little on edge about the visit, Rosa having talked about it as if its main purpose was to show her where she lived and introduce her to her mother. True, Rosa had said she'd arranged to meet up with Sylvia and Giada in the early evening, but this would just be for coffee before returning for dinner with her mother. So as Jeannie arrives at the station, she consoles herself with the thought that between now and meeting up with Silvia and Giada they'll have the rest of the afternoon to look around old Naples.

But this is not what happens.

Rosa is waiting at the station. As they leave, she tells Jeannie that Silvia won't be meeting up with them this evening because she's gone away to see her boyfriend. She also explains why Sylvia wasn't at the excavation for the second half of the week, having been suffering with a toothache. About Giada's absence she is less forthcoming, saying only that she's been unwell.

Jeannie would like to say, 'You don't have to give me an explanation, Rosa. I don't blame them for not coming,' and she's distracted by wondering whether she should say this as they board a city bus. She wants to ask where they're going, but the bus moves off quickly, and it's crowded, so she has to wait until they've jostled their way to seats either side of the aisle, by which time Rosa is telling her that her mother is a wonderful cook and makes fresh ricotta at least twice a week.

Without the advantage of a window seat Jeannie is struggling to see where they're going, that is until they come into a street where the bus stops and a name appears on a wall telling her this is Via di Tribunali. She recalls from last night's reading that this is one of the main streets of the centro storico, built over one of Naples' ancient roads and lined with arcaded buildings. She's trying to get the best view she can as Rosa begins to tell her about her late father. How he renovated their apartment but did not live long enough to enjoy it, dying of lung cancer, still a smoker to the end, and her mother lights one of his cigarettes in an ashtray to make the apartment smell of his presence on the anniversary of his death. Rosa adds, unnecessarily, that her mother treats the apartment as a shrine. Guessing that the apartment is the place they're now heading to, Jeannie makes a determined effort to halt their progress, saying, 'Oh, look, Rosa, there's an interesting church.' She pauses just long enough to give Rosa the chance to see the church, intending to add: 'I'd like to take a look,' but Rosa's glance towards the church is accompanied by, 'Oh, that is only Saint Paolo Maggiore. The church you really should see is the Duomo.'

Optimistically Jeannie says, 'Can we stop and take a look at that?'

'The Duomo is two blocks back,' Rosa tells her.

Then, to compound Jeannie's frustration as they trundle on, Rosa begins to explain why the Duomo is of such great importance. 'The Duomo was dedicated to Saint Gennaro, murdered just outside the city in 305 AD. Two phials of his blood were kept and when his body was transferred to the Duomo the blood in the phials liquefied in the bishop's hands. Since then, the miracle has been repeated three times a year. Failure of the blood to liquefy is a sign of disaster, as in 1944 – the last time Vesuvius erupted.'

Jeannie decides the best thing she can do is to appear to be giving Rosa her full attention whilst at the same time keeping an eye out for a café close to a bus stop where she'll suggest they get off for coffee. She's also trying to make a mental note of the route the bus is taking because this area looks worth coming back to.

As they come into Via Port Alba, Rosa begins to describe her extended family, talking mainly about her mother's sister, Aunt

Chiara, and Jeannie still hasn't spotted a suitable café. But she can see that the street ahead opens into what looks like a piazza, and she's sure there'll be cafés there. However, just before they turn into Piazza Dante, Rosa mentions that she's put out the photograph albums which have a record of four generations of her family. This instantly arouses Jeannie's interest, and as the city bus makes its way round the piazza Jeannie abandons the search for a café.

They get off the bus in Piazza Carita, and, as they walk towards the Spanish Quarter, Rosa tells her they live in one of the better insulae. Better or worse, all the insulae are of interest to Jeannie. Her reading about Naples has told her that this quarter is the nearest thing to ancient Rome, with its narrow streets, its clothes drying on lines strung between the old buildings, the many small ground-floor shops with crowded tenements above, and, most of striking of all, the graffiti on the walls and doors.

The greeting Rosa's mother gives Jeannie is effusive. She grips her hand between her own and speaks at length, looking from Jeannie to her daughter. The words 'famigliare' and 'famiglia' are often repeated and when Rosa's mother – whose actual name is not mentioned during the entire visit – has finished, she makes a rotating gesture with her forefinger; this to ask Rosa to translate what she's just said. The translation is much shorter than the original, Rosa explaining that her mother had said that she, Jeannie, looks like her sister, Aunt Chiara, when she was younger. Rosa adds that her mother said that Jeannie could be mistaken for one of the family.

When Rosa's mother next speaks she makes several nodding gestures towards Jeannie, then invites her daughter to translate.

This time Rosa fixes her eyes on Jeannie, as if to say, 'Please listen carefully.' Then she tells her: 'Mother has repeated what she just said. She wants to know that you are pleased because you are like her younger sister when she was the same age as you are now.'

So Jeannie says, 'Si? Grazie, grazie,' with a big smile.

Rosa's mother smiles back, and nods, and asks, through Rosa, if Jeannie would like tea or coffee. Taking the opportunity to practise her still limited Italian, Jeannie says, 'Un espresso al latte, per favore.' Rosa's mother smiles back, nods, and goes into the kitchen. Rosa then takes Jeannie to her bedroom. It has twin beds, and she invites Jeannie to put her bag on the one nearest the door, saying 'That was Caterina's.'

'Caterina?'

'Yes, my sister.'

'She no longer lives here?'

'Caterina has not stayed here since she qualified as a lawyer and went to work in Rome.'

'What, you mean she's not been home since then?'

'She has visited perhaps two or three times in six years but she stays in a hotel. On her company's expense, she tells us.'

Rosa clearly doubts that her sister's law firm would pay these bills, and Jeannie is tempted to enquire about why Caterina's doesn't want to stay here. But she thinks this too intrusive and offers instead, 'Well, at least you get to see her.'

'Yes,' is all Rosa says as she takes the pile of photograph albums from her bed. 'These are the family photographs,' she tells Jeannie, leading her back to the apartment's congested living room, where she puts the albums down on the sofa, inviting Jeannie to sit beside her.

Before they have the chance to look at the albums – and Jeannie does not want to reveal how keen she is to inspect them – Rosa's mother comes in with the coffee and what looks like a cheesecake.

'It is what I think you would call a moist ricotta cake,' Rosa tells Jeannie as her mother gives her a generous helping. Rosa adds, 'The café where we will meet Giada also has snacks. But we will have dinner at eight, so after this I will have nothing more until then.'

Having in mind the long gap between now and dinner, Jeannie expresses a great liking for 'la torta' when she's asked, via Rosa, if she likes it. She also returns some of Rosa's mother's nods. Her reward is another piece of the truly delicious torta, though this helping is a good bit smaller than the first. When Rosa's mother seems satisfied that Jeannie has genuinely enjoyed her cooking, she asks Rosa to tell her something: 'My mother wants you to know that in the south, Italian cooking is very straightforward. Further north it becomes more complicata.'

'Ah, further north – il nord – more complicata!' Jeannie acknowledges.

'Si si,' Rosa's mother says, adding, in her own version of pidgin Italian, 'A complicata, il nord, a complicata,' before she leaves the room.

In her absence Jeannie takes the opportunity to find out more about Rosa's mother, asking if she'd been a chef. 'No no!' Rosa says, 'Mother did not work outside the home after she had children. She gets her ideas about cooking from the television.'

'Si si, la televisione,' says her mother, returning to the lounge at that moment, laughing as she picks up their plates. In returning to the kitchen she cheerfully repeats, 'Si si, la televisione' several times over.

They settle into looking at the photographs, Rosa putting the top album of the pile in Jeannie's lap, taking the next one for herself. Jeannie has her own reason for wanting to inspect these family photographs and asks Rosa if she'll show her a photograph of her and Caterina when they were children. Rosa is pleased that Jeannie is interested in the photographs of her and her sister and when they've pored over a page of pictures of the two girls together with their mother and father, Jeannie remarks that Rosa looks more like her mother than does Caterina. She adds, 'Caterina looks more like your father.'

'Yes,' says Rosa, turning back several pages of the album she's holding to show Jeannie a page of photographs of her father.

'Your father and Caterina have some very distinctive features. I wonder which side of your father's family they come from?' says Jeannie.

In this way, over the next hour or so, a comprehensive picture of the features of the different sides of Rosa's family emerges. There are certain characteristics – the shapes of noses, low hairlines, full lips, and well sculptured cheekbones – which pick out Rosa and Caterina as distinctly different, and these features can be seen coursing through the generations. This contrasts with Jeannie's experience of trawling through her own family's photograph albums and looking for signs of the 'squaw's' features cascading through the generations. Jeannie is left thinking how remarkable it is that the kinds of genes that have expressed themselves so clearly in the different sides of Rosa's family had been unexpressed in so many generations of her own. She's still thinking about this when Rosa says, 'We should go now, or we will be late for Giada.'

Jeannie gets up from the sofa, taking the impressions of Rosa's family with her.

The café, in a quiet street off Via Toledo, is a good walk from Rosa's apartment. Giada is waiting, looking downcast, avoiding eye contact with Jeannie for the first few minutes. Rosa repeats her explanation that Giada had a heavy cold last week and wasn't well enough to be at the excavation. She adds that Giada is still feeling down because of the cold's after-effects. But it's soon apparent that her unhappiness is for a quite different reason.

Not long into their faltering conversation, Giada says, 'Naples is a dump.'

Jeannie is surprised to hear this phrase coming from someone whose English is so shaky, and Rosa takes it upon herself to explain that Giada's boyfriend has left Naples to work in Perugia, and he's not been in contact for the last week. Giada then takes up the story in staccato, searching Jeannie's eyes with each short line delivered:

'We were at school, the same.'

'We write email all the time.'

'He returns after one month.'

'He is not the same.'

'There was no reply to the email I send him last week.'

'He has a girl... in Perugia... you think?'

Giada and Rosa wait for a reply and Jeannie feels hemmed in. It seems she's being put in the role of Agony Aunt, and it occurs to her that consultations about relationships are the real reason she's been invited for this stay in Naples. She tentatively offers: 'Maybe your boyfriend needs some time – some space – to sort himself out. If he'd been definite about wanting to break things off he would have emailed to say so. That's my guess. So there's hope in not knowing – and it's probably best not to chase him.'

There is no immediate response from either Giada or Rosa, and it's clear this is not the desired answer. Jeannie is tempted to say that they'll soon be back in college, as if to suggest there are more fish in the sea, but in remembering her mother's attempt at similar consolation after she'd been dumped by Alex, she decides against this, offering only silence.

'You think that?' is all Giada says before she leaves.

After she's gone Rosa apologises for her friend's rudeness and suggests they return for dinner with her mother. On the way back Rosa mentions that her boyfriend is also in Perugia, at university, but he doesn't know the boy Giada is going out with. Jeannie assumes that Rosa mentioning her boyfriend is the opener to have a consultation about him, and, to head this off, she asks questions about virtually every other building they pass as they walk along Via Toledo.

Rosa's mother's cooking is amazing, but the evening is slow and tedious as she insists on Rosa translating everything that's said. And she drinks the red wine freely. Each time she gets up to go to the kitchen she laughs and repeats one of her earlier remarks: 'A complicata, il nord, a complicata!' Or: 'Si si. La televisione!'

By nine thirty it's apparent that Rosa's mother is quite drunk.

When the meal is over Rosa tells her mother she'll clear up

and make coffee for Jeannie. She suggests that her mother goes to watch television, and she does so without fuss.

Whilst they're clearing up, Jeannie asks Rosa if her mother is often like this. 'No no,' Rosa replies, 'she is only like this on Saturdays. It is the family meal we always had together. It is her way of dealing with my father's death.'

In the lounge Rosa's mother is sleeping soundly in front of the television. Rosa turns the sound down so it can hardly be heard. She fetches a blanket and places it over her mother. She whispers to tell Jeannie that her mother will wake in two or three hours and take herself to bed.

It's now a little after ten-thirty and Rosa asks if Jeannie is tired. Jeannie has first use of the bathroom, then she gets into Caterina's bed. She switches off the bedside light, feeling really tired, and she's almost asleep by the time Rosa comes in. So, with closed eyes, Jeannie does not see how pleased Rosa is to have her to herself. And Rosa seems to think that Jeannie is waiting with closed eyes and bated breath to hear her whispers.

'Alfredo, that is my boyfriend, is handsome in the Italian way. We were at the same school, he is two years older, and we only started dating the year before he went to university. He has now started to prepare for his finals, and that is why he does not come home very often.'

Jeannie hears this, though there seems to be a time lag between the words being uttered and their sinking in. And for some reason she feels the need to ask where Alfredo is at university.

'In Perugia,' Rosa whispers proudly, 'it is one of the best.'

'Oh, yes... Perugia... you told me,' Jeannie just about manages to say. Though Jeannie's mind is beginning to drift, she's sufficiently awake to remember that Giada's boyfriend is also in Perugia, and she wonders if Giada has asked if Rosa's boyfriend could find out what's going on. She's about to make the effort to ask Rosa this, but Rosa has already started saying, 'This summer, we met at his house, when Alfredo's parents were on holiday, and there were times when I wanted to be his.'

Rosa pauses long enough for Jeannie to think she's been left in peace, but no, Rosa adds: 'What do you think?'

'What do I think? What do I think ... What do I think about what?' is the thought Jeannie's mind is trying to process. Then she hears again, '...there were times when I wanted to be his...' and she's not sure if Rosa has repeated this or whether the words are an echo in her head, but she's able to open her eyes for long enough to find Rosa looking at her intently, and she's definitely saying: 'Do you think I should give myself to Alfredo?'

Jeannie is vaguely aware that she may be smiling at the words she's thinking. And she's not at all sure that these words are actually passing her lips, but she's trying very hard to say: 'He'd come home more often if you did.'

The next morning Jeannie wakes up early. She's just had a dream in which Rosa's mother, dressed in Rosa's long dressing gown, has wrestled her to the kitchen floor to prevent her from leaving. The perturbing effect of this dream is still with her when she showers.

Rosa's mother is already up and busy in the kitchen, but she does not offer Jeannie anything to eat or drink when she goes in to see her. Instead, through use of the single word 'bambina' and gesticulation, Rosa's mother indicates that Rosa will be left to have her sleep out. Jeannie drinks cold water from the bathroom tap, then goes back to the kitchen to mime to Rosa's mother, using both hands and one foot, to tell her that she's going out for a walk. She leaves the apartment building hoping to find somewhere to get a cup of coffee, and perhaps a pastry, but it's far too early. It doesn't cross her mind to take this opportunity to have a look round the poorer parts of Quartieri Spagnoli. And if it had, she would have likely dismissed the idea since what she wants to see is the area when it's buzzing with people.

Without finding anywhere open, she returns to Rosa's mother's apartment feeling irritably out of sorts. Rosa is at the small table in the kitchen, sleepily sipping coffee with a glass of water. It's not until Rosa's mother comes in that Jeannie is offered the same and Rosa tells her that they don't normally eat breakfast, but she can have some ham and fruit if she wishes. Jeannie wants to leave as soon as possible, so she asks for coffee with milk, deciding this will have to do for breakfast.

When Rosa's mother leaves the kitchen Jeannie tells Rosa that she needs to get back to the hostel, explaining that she needs to spend the day on her research. Rosa says she'll come with her to the bus stop after she's had a shower, so the next twenty minutes are passed in an intermittent mimed conversation with Rosa's mother in the kitchen. It may be that this is about the weather, or the view of the neighbours from the window. It's hard to tell, but the saving grace is that Rosa's mother doesn't mention 'la televisione' or 'il nord, a complicata'.

By the time they get to the bus stop, Rosa having several times tried to start a conversation about Alfredo, Jeannie is feeling quite grizzly. Then, when the bus is in sight, and Rosa is still pressing Jeannie for an answer to the question 'Should I?' Jeannie can't help but speak plainly:

'Rosa, one way or another, your mother needs to know that you're a woman now.'

Jeannie gets on the bus, leaving Rosa looking like she's just tasted the soft centre of a rather tart fruit pastille.

Less than ten minutes later, her city map telling her the next stop is the one that's nearest the museum, Jeannie gets off the bus. She makes her way to the museum, expecting that it won't open until late on a Sunday, only to find it opens at nine and has a catering service.

Something resembling the irritation of Sunday morning is picked up first thing on Monday. And it begins as a repeat experience. The door to the scroll workshop is open as it was the week before, and Angus is poking through the rejected scrolls in the cabinet at the rear of the cabin.

Jeannie says, 'Good morning'. Without turning, or returning her greeting, he says, 'The next lot of students should have turned up at the hostel yesterday.'

'Yes, they all turned up, except one whose plane was delayed.'

'Right, good. They're due on site at ten.'

She puts her sandwich bag down close to the outlet of the air conditioning unit and waits until he's finished what he's doing. When he turns, he says, 'Right, I've sorted out four scrolls that can be unpicked some more. I'll have all the students on site today to show them what we're doing and to get them started. From tomorrow I want you to have four students at a time, one day per group, to take them through what we do in here. All right?'

'Yes,' she says.

'Right, and if you could spend no more than an hour with them, just to show them the ropes, then leave them to it and get back to supervising the sorting and sifting.'

'Right,' she says, withholding the 'sir' that's come to mind.

'I'd like you at the induction at ten, which we'll do outside the site office,' he says as he leaves.

Having in mind the care taken by the body-cavity lady only last Friday, to provide the students with an archaeological learning experience, what Angus is up to looks increasingly like sheer exploitation. And what Jeannie finds most unpalatable is that she's being roped in as his taskmaster. Until they've taken the site down by as much as another metre and a half, they're unlikely to find anything of interest. The work of this batch of students, possibly for the whole of their site placement, will likely consist of removing ash and pumice crumble in which nothing more than roof tiles and carbonised roof trusses are embedded. All this to be done as quickly as possible to enable Angus and Simply Elaine to resume their search for the Rembrandt in the attic – and achieve fame by it.

Or so it seems to Jeannie.

So as she walks to the site office she's wondering how Angus will motivate this year's final crop of students. And, over the eight-week period of their site placement, how he'll sustain it.

The students, less the one who's been delayed, are already

gathered by the site office when she gets there. Angus and Giorgio are in front of the students and she is obliged to join them.

Angus says, 'Right, we're a bit early but let's make a start.' He welcomes the students, saying he's going to kick off by telling them the basics: they should be on site by eight; there are tea and coffee making facilities in the site office; there's also a fridge for their sandwiches and drinks, and the portable toilets are there (he points). He then introduces himself as 'the chief archaeologist on site' and Giorgio as 'my deputy here'. Jeannie is named as his 'first assistant'. His first joke may be ironic in that he tells his eager audience, 'You'll learn a lot more from what we say than what we do!'

The students know this is a joke because Angus is laughing as he says it.

He then begins his motivational talk. 'You are the third group of archaeology students on site. The first group did the outlying work to confirm we had a villa of importance here. They began to excavate the street and villa frontage, which we'll show you in a minute. The second group completed the excavation of the frontage and undertook the clearance of the villa's outer perimeter before making a start on the area under cover. Your work is to take us to the heart of the matter...' Jeannie listens as he continues, noting the technique in his words: 'It's you, the present group of students, who'll drive the excavation to what really matters, which is what life here was like, and it's likely we'll find more body cavities.'

Jeannie hopes this is not the case, at least not as far as the slave-scribe is concerned, as a buzz of excitement goes round a group now eager to start their work. But Angus does not release them at this moment. Rather in the manner of a true showman he holds them back to give them notice of their treat. 'It's not the only thing we have for you. You'll also get to spend a whole day working on the carbonised scrolls you'll have read about in the briefing notes I sent you.'

Giorgio leads his group of students to the marked-off area at the back of the excavation, and Jeannie follows. She's accompanied by the slim Japanese girl who introduced herself yesterday evening by her nickname, 'Kimono', and she's keen to talk. 'I feel so privileged to be here at this stage of the excavation. I think Dr Angus must think this a very important site for him to come all the way from England to supervise it.'

'Yes,' Jeannie says, 'this is an important site, and for all sorts of reasons.'

'Yes, I think so.'

'Of course it's bound to be hard work at this stage of the dig.'

'Sure, I understand that. Dr Angus said this in his letter to us.'

By eleven on their first morning the students are working hard and the process of taking down the dig is going well. At five-thirty they return to the hostel as a single group, invigorated by hard work. At seven Jeannie leads them to the café-restaurant, where the tables and chairs are set out as usual. Kimono makes sure to sit next to Jeannie and asks her lots of questions about Britain. From what she asks, and from what she says, it's apparent that she's already well informed about Jeannie's home country, although she's never been there.

Thursday. After their fourth day on site the students make their way to the café-restaurant in their own small groups. Kimono comes to Jeannie's room and seems intent on keeping her talking. Jeannie finds this a little odd, and a little later she thinks it strange that only she and Kimono are making their way to their evening meal. All is explained, however, as they enter the café restaurant. The tables are now arranged in a U shape. Angus and Giorgio are at the bar beneath a painted banner which has 'HAPPY BIRTHDAY JEANNIE' written on it.

Jeannie is caught by surprise, having completely lost track of the date. She's also puzzled as to how they knew it was her birthday, since she'd forgotten about it and not mentioned it to anyone. But there's no time to enquire about this as the students surge forward to congratulate her, then step aside for Angus to present her with the card they've all signed.

It's not until everyone is moving to a seat on the outside of the U-shaped arrangement of tables that Jeannie has the chance to ask Giorgio how Angus knew about her birthday. Giorgio treats this whispered question as a moment of intimacy, whispering back, 'He does things like this. He looks at the form you fill in when you come to work here, and then we have one of his parties. You will see how it is.'

By the time Giorgio has said this he's grinning.

As Jeannie reaches her seat at the centre of the arrangement of tables, Angus is announcing that he'll be paying for the meal, and they've got a special menu tonight. 'But we'll have to club together to buy the drinks,' he adds. Upon hearing this the students give a loud cheer.

The atmosphere is festive, the meal enjoyable, and no one notices Angus go into the toilets as the tables are being cleared. Neither does anyone seem to notice that the chef has joined the barman and waiter behind the bar. It's not until Angus emerges from the toilet that the whole party – except Giorgio – gasp at his well-kept secret. He's dressed in full Highlander kit and when he reaches what now looks like the disco area, at the head of the U-shape of tables, he takes a bow. He then turns and goes to the bar to receive what turns out to be a pair of claymores wrapped in a tartan blanket, formally handed to him jointly by the barman and waiter. Back at the disco area, standing erect and holding his tartan bundle, he's also looking rather overdressed – and hot. Knowing the short jacket he's wearing to be quite heavy, Jeannie thinks it would be best if he removed it, but she's in no position to say this and anyway Angus has commenced his performance, revealing the claymores. The students gasp at each sword's appearance, and then there's a murmur of excitement as Angus places them in a cross on the floor before him. He then stands erect, as if composing himself, and this is the cue for the barman to turn on the tape recorder perched on the bar. The slightly muffled recording of a Highland tune once used to sell a particular brand of porridge oats now fills the room: *Dar da da-dar,dar-dar-dar,da-dar, da-dar, da- dar dar, da-dar- dar, dar-da-da....*

Angus is at first unmoved, again emphasising his upright posture, but this time as if in homage to the scratchy tune. Then, with a single leap, he's straddling the Claymore blades with quickly moving feet. The barman and chef lead the clapping and whooping, and encouraged by this, on every third step Angus makes an emphatic upward movement of the knee. It's as if trying to flick the sporran towards his upright head, offering the tantalising prospect of revealing what's beneath his kilt. Soon the emphasis of all the clapping and whooping is on this third step. Encouraged by this, Angus makes every effort to send his sporran ever upwards whilst nimbly treading the space between the Claymores. But it's soon apparent that he's the victim of too many good lunches at his favourite restaurant in Naples as beads of perspiration break out on his forehead. His posture soon becomes a little stooped, and a quick glance up at his audience suggests he'd like to give up this self-inflicted suffering. But the students are well into his performance and clap more furiously than before.

Jeannie glances in Giorgio's direction. His fist is in his mouth and tears are running down his cheeks. She wonders if she shouldn't somehow intervene to stop Angus doing himself some harm, but she needn't worry, for a second later Angus suddenly stops, head down, putting up a hand to say he's done for.

The students clap even more furiously at his final pose, and led by Kimono – who seems very slightly built as she approaches – they crowd around Angus to pat him from every angle.

Jeannie, now a spectator at her own party, finds herself approached by Giorgio, who puts an arm around her shoulder to give her a birthday kiss on the cheek. She accepts this, but when he continues to hold her, with the smell of wine sweet on his breath, she tries to pull away, saying, 'Giorgio, you're drunk.'

'I know, is your birthday,' he says, as if the two facts are inextricably linked.

Jeannie pokes her fingers into his side to get him to release her, at the same time saying, 'You're not driving home, are you?' She immediately realises he will take this as an invitation to stay with her in the hostel, and sure enough he whispers: 'I stay with you, then.'

'No,' she says, 'I don't think so.'

Still the grinning drunk Giorgio steps back, pointing to Angus's admirers as if to say, 'Ok, one of these will do then.'

It's possible that the two elderly volunteers at the excavation, who make it a habit of being invisible, have been watching. They're referred to as Tweedledum and Tweedledee by the students – this naming almost certainly having been passed on by Angus and Giorgio – and they take it in turns to offer their birthday congratulations to Jeannie in flawless English, to say what a nice party it's been, to add how much they've enjoyed the entertainment. They give the time of the next train as their reason for leaving.

Though their departure seems unnoticed, it's as if it's the cue for the party to end, the students going back to the hostel as a single group soon after. After thanking Angus for the party, Jeannie hurries to catch them. Kimono is leading the conversation as Jeannie joins them. 'Ah, Jeannie, we were just saying how amazing it is that Dr Angus does the dance with the swords!'

'Yes, amazing, isn't it.'

'The clothes he is wearing, that is the national dress of Scotland, I think?'

'Yes, it is.'

'But he is from England, is that correct?'

'He is, but his father is a Scot.'

'You really are from Scotland, aren't you?'

'Yes.'

'And do you wear a kilt also?'

'Well not exactly. The equivalent for a woman is a plaid skirt. I had one when I was about seven. If I wore it now, it would be like a mini.'

Kimono's eyes light up. 'You hear that everyone! Jeannie had a kilt when she was little, now it will be a mini-skirt if she wears it!' The group halts as Kimono adds, 'Jeannie, I think it would be fantastic if you wear your kilt with bright red tights, and those big bother boots. Or better, you have no tights and have tattoos on your legs. That would be fantastic!'

Still as a single group they enter the hostel, dispersing in their various directions from the stairwell. Jeannie, at the back of the group on the first-floor landing, does not at first see the shoebox that's been left on the floor against her door. As she stoops to pick it up, she's sure she can guess its contents. In her room, having locked the door behind her, she puts the box down on her small desk. Then she stands back, pausing for a moment before taking her toothbrush and tweezers from their place on the vanity unit. She's still standing when she lifts the lid of the box, but she's seated when she gently divides the loose ash and pumice which has not been subject to compression whilst in its hidden niche at the top of the wall in the scribe's room. The toothbrush handle and blunt end of the tweezers are sufficient for her to do her work, and she soon discovers five tightly rolled scrolls together with something completely unexpected: a carbonised wooden tablet the size of a playing card on which the words are clearly visible when she holds the tablet beneath her desk light.

The words, in Ancient Greek, stand out as if she alone were meant to read them.

I, slave-scribe to
Asinius, have killed
him so that I might
have my own life.

Rufus Mettius
Diomedes

Her first thought is that this might explain the fracture on Asinius' skull. This not, it seems, caused by a falling roof tile, or piece of masonry, as Dr Lilia of the body-cavity preservation team had mentioned. Her first instinct is to put the tablet back between the scrolls in the shoebox, to return it to Giorgio tomorrow and ask him to put its contents back where he found them. At the same time to make it clear to Giorgio – just in case there's any lingering doubt – that his proposition, in all its aspects, is not going to happen. Set against this is a strong desire to hang on to Rufus Mettius' carbonised tablet, as if to protect him. But recognising that this will deny Angus the knowledge of the name of both master and slave and that anyway, it would be totally improper to remove anything from the site for her own personal use, she carefully places the tablet back amongst the scrolls.

However, this does not bring the matter to a close and she sits back to consider why she's so tempted to make the tablet her own. It's soon clear to her what's going on here: she wants to find a good reason why Rufus Mettius would need to commit this homicidal act before it's made common knowledge to all on site, and to the world at large. And, yes, if she keeps the tablet safe until she finds such good reason, no harm will be done. As long, that is, as the tablet is returned to its proper place in due course. With this thought in mind Jeannie removes the tablet for a second time, taking it to the set of drawers beside the vanity unit and carefully placing it between her neatly ironed T-shirts, thinking, *Yes, this is the best course of action, for the moment.*

Friday goes well.

Although Giorgio is out of sorts – having spent the night in a sleeping bag on the floor of the site office – he's persuaded to discreetly put the scrolls back in the niche where they belong. And having parted with the slave-scribe's scrolls, Jeannie decides she'll talk to Angus about them first thing on Monday morning. She'll tell him she has a hunch that the scrolls will be of interest, and possibly the subject of her research.

She then puts these thoughts aside.

By lunchtime the last group of this intake of students has gone through the scroll workshop, every student having unpicked the requisite length of scroll and transcribed it. After providing her translation of their transcripts, Jeannie returns to the excavation with them, now optimistic that the dig will soon give up more of its treasures. This quite radical change of outlook, this new optimism about the excavation providing valuable information is, she knows, down to just one thing: her sense that Rufus Mettius escaped the eruption and she'll soon have the chance to read the scrolls he left behind.

At the weekend, on Saturday, she visits Herculaneum. It's fascinating to walk round the excavated part of this small ancient city. Even more so to see its buildings emerging from the cliff face of soft sedimentary rock that was once a' gigantic wave of displaced mud and sand as Vesuvius tipped millions of tons of ash and pumice into the sea. But what's so striking to Jeannie is the absence of artefacts in the rooms of the houses – the ones she'd seen in the repository in Naples. And she imagines being in these rooms with these objects reinstated, with people clothed exactly as they were and behaving exactly as they did. What registers in her imagination is that these people were us.

First thing on Sunday morning, in her own time, she goes over to the scroll workshop. She goes straight to the storage cabinet and takes the four scrolls Angus had put out for this batch of students to unpick, her intention being to complete the unpicking of them and then copy the translation of each onto her laptop. In doing this, she'll be able to see what Asinius actually said at his all-male dinner parties, as recorded in Rufus Mettius's hand, and how this was altered and added to by Asinius. In this way she'll be able to see the how the finished scripts – Asinius' own scrolls – were transformed. That is, she'll be able to see how Asinius emerged as a storyteller of great stature, a loquacious wit and the embodiment of all that's wise. It's in doing this that Jeannie comes to the conclusion that Rufus Mettius, whose presence at these dinner parties was not acknowledged, must have found this whole business really tedious.

In the afternoon Jeannie goes to the beach with Kimono and some of the other students, and whilst returning to the hostel the prospect of destroying Rufus Mettius's cache of scrolls by unpicking them fills her with a sense of horror. So she decides that first thing on Monday, as well as telling Angus about her interest in the slave scribe's scrolls, she'll also tell him she has an interest in finding a non-destructive method of reading the scrolls, as Professor Dinsdale had suggested.

Monday: it's a little before nine, and Jeannie is concerned about how Angus will take her proposal. She's certain he'll remind of her previous lack of interest in developing a non-destructive method of scroll reading, and she's decided to pass this off lightly, saying something like: 'I didn't realise its importance until I saw a whole scroll in tiny pieces.'

The little speech she intends to make is well rehearsed, but she's pre-empted by what Angus has to tell her. 'Professor Dinsdale rang me at home over the weekend,' he says. 'He reckons there's a company in Scotland's own Silicon Valley who may be able to read scrolls electronically. What do you think about going back to find out?'

Jeannie's immediate thought is not to sound too keen, and certainly not to rush into putting forward the scribe's scrolls for this purpose. So she says, 'Well, yes, that sounds interesting. But what about my work here?'

'Now the students have got the hang of the dig they could do the sorting and sifting themselves, couldn't they? It's not as if anything of much interest is likely to turn up in this layer of the excavation.'

'No, I suppose not,' she says, after a pause, hoping her hesitation sounds genuine.

'Listen,' Angus says, handing her the coffee he's just made, 'if a non-destructive method of reading the scrolls can be found, the director might be persuaded to let us resume removing the scrolls from the scriptorium.'

'So you'd like me to take some of the scrolls back to Scotland, to see if they can be read?'

'I thought you were interested in the scrolls Giorgio says are hidden in the scribe's room.'

'Yes, well I am, sort of. I just thought that if there were scrolls written by a slave-scribe, and hidden, they might tell us something about how the other half lived.'

'Yes, well, that's fine with me.'

Chapter 4

A Brief Encounter

Jeannie's unease about staying with her parents comes into her mind the moment she calls her mother from Glasgow Airport. She tells her mother where she is, and that she'll be coming straight home, if that's all right. Surprised to hear that she's back in Scotland, her mother is concerned that something untoward has happened and, in truth, Jeannie knows she should have let her know in advance that she was coming home, if only the day before. But in her haste to take possession of Rufus Mettius's scrolls, and making sure not to forget to bring his tablet which she has been keeping in the drawer with her T-shirts, and the time it took to book a flight, not forgetting the roster she had to make to rotate the students round the sorting and sifting, she did not give phoning her mother a second thought. So, she tries to reassure her that nothing's wrong, telling her that the decision to return to do some specialised work in the university labs was made only yesterday: this is untrue by twenty-four hours.

Her mother says, 'Oh well, that's fine then,' but there's a catch in her voice which suggests she doesn't quite believe her daughter.

Back home her mother greets her with a kiss and says, 'Jeannie you're looking so thin.' Taking her hands and turning them palm up, she says, 'They're so callused, what have you been doing?'

Jeannie explains that finding a body cavity at the excavation has meant that the whole site needs to be excavated as a piece, with no more exploratory trenches, and work for the last few weeks has just been hard digging. Her mother looks uneasy at the mention of a body cavity, and isn't at all curious to know the details, but mainly she seems placated by what Jeannie tells her. Indeed, she smiles and gives Jeannie the old cliché, 'Well, a bit of hard work never did anyone any harm.'

Reassured, she then begins to ask the expected questions: What's the accommodation like? Are the other people nice? Have you met anyone yet? Jeannie is able to reassure her mother on the first two points but not the last, saying: 'There are some good-looking students, but they're too young.'

'Aye,' her mother affirms, 'I suppose you'd like someone a wee bit older.'

She then tells Jeannie she must get on with dinner. Jeannie's offer of help is accepted and the visit home looks like it has got off to a promising start. But when her mother notices the unfamiliar small ribbed aluminium case Jeannie has left with her bags in the hallway, her tone changes.

'What's that?' she asks.

'It's a case we use to carry the artefacts,' Jeannie begins, and making the mistake of thinking her mother will be interested in its contents – and her work – she goes on to say, 'It's got five scrolls in it, written, we think, by a slave-scribe. I've brought them back to see if we can get them electronically read without the need to unpick and destroy them. I've also got a tablet the scribe wrote, saying he killed his master.'

Her mother's thoughts focus on just one thing: 'Killed his master, did you say? Oh, Jeannie, I don't think I want that in the house.'

'I'll take it to my room, it'll be gone by tomorrow – I'll be taking it to the university labs,' Jeannie tells her quickly.

She breaks off from helping her mother in the kitchen to take her bags and the aluminium case up to her bedroom. In her room she wonders if perhaps she's expecting too much of a mother whose life outside the home has never consisted of more than two half-days a week of voluntary work in a charity shop. And she wonders if the aluminium case is associated in her mother's mind with the metal case she'd found in her late grandfather's attic, the contents of which explained where her daughter's alien looks had come from.

Determined to make a fresh start with her mother, Jeannie goes downstairs to resume helping prepare dinner. Intending to do everything to be polite and patient, she gets the vegetables ready. It's clear that her mother won't let her anywhere near the meat, this being her mother's province, and Jeannie accepts this. All looks like being well as they work together, but her mother keeps coming back to the same question: 'How long will you be staying?'

It's not that her mother wants her to stay for a particular length of time, two weeks rather than three, for instance. It's just that it's a thing she needs to know for her peace of mind. And it's as if by repeating the same question, though with some rephrasing, she will get a definite answer out of her daughter.

Finally, her patience almost exhausted, Jeannie tells her: 'Mum, I'll be at home for a few days at the most. After that the travelling will be too much and I'll find temporary accommodation in Glasgow until the work on the scrolls is finished.'

Her mother's reply does not surprise her: 'Oh, Jeannie, you can stay as long as you like.'

Jeannie waits until the time she's been told Professor Dinsdale normally arrives at his office, which is 9.30. She gives it a few minutes longer, to be sure to catch him. Then she makes her phone call. She's given some thought to what she'll tell him but doesn't get the chance to say anything. 'Ah, Jeannie, it's you. Yes, Angus rang. I've got you in my diary for 2.30, so you can tell me all about what's going on at the excavation when I see you.'

She decides to go straight into Glasgow, intending to see if there's a place in the B&B hotel in Kelvingrove where she'd stayed whilst searching for a bed-sit two years earlier. But before leaving home there's something she needs to do. Under her bed is a cardboard box, inside which is the brown paper parcel her mother discovered in her late grandfather's attic. Jeannie pulls the box onto the carpet and kneeling over it, she carefully lifts the lid and removes the parcel. From this she takes the moccasins and mittens and delves further to find the silver print photograph and the once screwed-up note saying Archie wanted the boys returned to Scotland. Satisfied that the parcel's contents are exactly as she last saw them, she returns them to the folds of brown paper together with Rufus Mettius's carbonised tablet. She carefully replaces the parcel in its box and returns this to the space beneath her bed.

Concerned to be punctual, she arrives ten minutes early. Professor Dinsdale's secretary asks her to take a seat in her office, which has a waiting area. It's strange, Jeannie thinks, but she has no recollection of this waiting area and his secretary working in one corner. She must have been quite nervous when she came to the so-called interview, she now realises. As if to make up for this, she casts her eye about the room to see what she missed. Professor Dinsdale's secretary is clattering away at the keyboard of what looks like a very out-of-date tower computer. One of the filing cabinets is new, and Jeannie thinks it's a pity they didn't replace the other two battered specimens when adding this one. Yes, a new filing cabinet at either side of the secretary's desk, plus a new computer, would sort the office out quite nicely.

She's been there for perhaps a quarter of an hour, expecting Professor Dinsdale to walk in any moment, when she decides to have a look at the book on the coffee table. The light reflecting from its glossy surface has prevented her from reading the title, but when she picks it up she discovers it's about Scottish settlers in Canada. Surprised by this, and eager to see if it has anything to say about the native people, she's just beginning to have a read when the professor arrives. He apologises for his lateness and asks her to go into his office. Whilst she waits there he has a long and annoyingly out of earshot conversation with his secretary.

It's the best part of ten minutes before he joins Jeannie and he begins by reminding her that Angus rang. He goes on to tell her about what's going on at the scavi, making it sound as if it's he, not she, who's been working there.

'So,' he concludes, 'I'm up to date with what's been happening.'

This adds irritation to annoyance. And when he says, 'There's a certain company in our own Silicon Valley which, I'm told, does work for a certain government department,' she'd like to say: 'that's the third time I've been told that,' but what's noticeable about the way he's saying this is that he is being theatrical, his forefinger touching the side of his nose as he mentions this 'certain company'. As he does this, Jeannie is struck by how much he looks like one of her mother's favourite characters in *Dad's Army*, the wild-eyed Scot played by John Laurie, whose eccentric glances seem to suggest a streak of lunacy running through the family. She dismisses this 'let's keep it a secret' nose-touching gesture as an attempt to heighten the drama.

'Is there?' she says, to fill the gap his pause has left.

'There is, there is,' he says, and adds, 'They'll need to be approached with, how shall I put it, due care and attention. But I'm sure you can do that.'

Jeannie tries to clarify exactly what he's saying. 'You mean they have the technology to electronically read a document contained within another, to read a letter through a sealed envelope for instance?'

Touching the side of his nose again, he coyly confides, 'Well, that's always a possibility.' Then, as if he's already said too much, he changes the subject. 'There's space in the larger of the teaching labs for you to do your work on cleaning up the scrolls you've brought with you. And, Jeannie, I think it would be best if you take responsibility for their safe keeping – at least for the moment.'

As he's saying this, he's glancing at the many papers spread across his desk, as if to suggest this interview is over. But there's something Jeannie needs to ask. 'Could you tell me if my application for a bursary includes travel expenses for return visits to the excavation?'

'Ah, good point,' he says, before calling, 'Margaret!' He turns to Jeannie to add in a whisper, 'Miss McBride will be able to tell us.'

Miss Margaret McBride bobs into the doorway.

'Did we include return travel expenses to Italy in Jeannie's bursary application?' he asks quite sternly, as if to let her know it's her fault if they didn't.

'I don't rightly know, I'll have to take a look,' she says before bobbing back. The drawer of a filing cabinet is heard to open, and Margaret McBride is soon back in the doorway, saying, 'No. We didn't.'

'Then would you add, what do you think Jeannie, three return visits per year?'

Jeannie is wondering whether this will be sufficient when Professor Dinsdale's secretary says, 'I will' and disappears back into her office as Dinsdale assures Jeannie, 'It's two weeks before the committee meets, so there's plenty of time to change your bursary application.' A moment later he says, 'If there's a delay before they can read your scrolls, assuming they can, and you've got time on your hands, it would be useful for you spend the time reading up on Pax Romana – you know, the hundred years of peace in the Roman Empire in which the Vesuvius eruption occurred.'

Jeannie's proposed research supervisor finally gives her an unequivocal signal that their meeting is over, saying: 'Miss

McBride will give you the details of the company you're to contact on your way out.'

In the outer office Margaret McBride is standing by her desk holding a white envelope marked CONFIDENTIAL. As Jeannie takes the envelope from her, she withdraws her hand as if she's released something that might be toxic. Noticing this, and thinking this cloak and dagger hush-hush stuff really rather silly, Jeannie has almost left the office before she remembers the glossy book on the coffee table.

'Is it all right if I take another look?' she says, pointing to the book.

'That's fine, but we close at four,' she's told.

Not wishing to be found there when Professor Dinsdale leaves, Jeannie leafs through the book as quickly as she can. She soon sees that it's a celebration of the success of many of Scotland's most well-known names. It illustrates the places they've settled in Canada and outlines their achievements in every walk of life. There are old photographs of the pioneers, some from Scotland's wealthier families and some from its poorest. For its large size, the book only has a very short introduction. Jeannie hopes it will say something about the native people, but Native North Americans have no mention.

Thinking she's close to finding out what Rufus Mettius has to say in his scrolls, Jeannie has become apprehensive lest they don't live up to expectations. She's dealing with this by telling herself that the idea that this man might represent the voice of all the unheard and unheard-of people is, in fact, a very tall order. She's also told herself that reading up on Pax Romana, as suggested by

Professor Dinsdale, will be very useful if she's to fully understand what Rufus Mettius has to say in his scrolls. In view of these two considerations, she's not going to hurry removing the ash and pumice clinging to the scrolls, and she's delaying contacting the hush-hush company in order to spend as much time as she can in the college library.

After almost a week of doing this, and having taken the best part of a day to move into the B&B hotel in Kelvingrove, she can delay no longer. The scrolls are ready.

They are of uniform size, and although carbonised you can tell they're written on the finest papyrus. They look exactly the same length as those accredited to Asinius and are tightly rolled. There's nothing on the outside that speaks of their content, nor of the sequence in which they were written, and she telephones her contact at the company whose name must be kept secret.

Their conversation is businesslike:

'Ah, hello, I'm an archaeology research student of Professor Dinsdale's here in Glasgow. He suggested I contact you.'

'About what exactly?'

'Well, I'm doing work on the carbonised scrolls recovered from a site in the Bay of Naples.'

'Carbonised scrolls? What are they exactly?'

'Well, Vesuvius erupted in 79 AD and during the last phase of the eruption, when the vast column of ash began to collapse, it forced an incredibly hot cloud of gas down the mountain and organic things like wood and papyrus were preserved by being instantly carbonised. I've been working on the carbonised scrolls recovered from a site between Pompeii and Herculaneum, we unpick the scrolls bit-by-bit to see what's written on them. The problem with this is...'

'You destroy the scrolls in the process.'

'Yes, exactly.'

'Well, you'd better come and see me. Do you know what the ink was made from?'

'No, but I can find out.'

'Yes, and you'll need to bring one of the scrolls to see if we can do anything for you.'

When Jeannie meets her mystery man, who can only be known as Mr X, it's clear that he finds her attractive, and the effect this has on his behaviour is obvious. He tries to get the formalities out of the way as quickly as he can. He tells Jeannie that if he takes on this project, then the only thing she'll be able to say in any paper she writes about the scrolls is that the research was supported by the parent company, which he names. She'll have to sign the Official Secrets Act, of course, and it would be a breach of the Act if she were to describe how she thought the scrolls were read or named the place. For these reasons he won't be saying anything about how it's done.

Having dispensed with the formalities he becomes chatty, asking about what she does at the excavation. The chance to explain what she's been up to, so far denied her since her return to Scotland, means that she's more than happy to tell him about her work. It's soon obvious where this chat is leading, even before he invites her to lunch at 'a nearby quaint old pub'. She's truthful when she says she's got a train to catch at 12.20. But, she adds, 'Perhaps the next time.'

On the train back to Glasgow she wonders why she said this; why she intimated that she might be interested. Was it to ensure the scrolls would be read, or was she really tempted? Maybe she was just flattered by the attention he gave her. It's difficult to know. He's a handsome man is Mr X and she likes the shape of his shoulders, but a wedding ring says he's married, and she has no intention of being another of his extra-marital conquests. Perhaps, she thinks, her reply was just the sort of thing you say to put off the moment of decision, but then again there was no need to say it.

She sees Professor Dinsdale to let him know it will be up to two weeks before she'll know if the scroll she left with the company can be read. If it can, it could be a further two weeks before the others can be similarly dealt with. She adds that she wonders if it might best for someone else were to deliver the remaining scrolls, if they can be read, and she return to Italy in the meantime.

Professor Dinsdale is decisive. 'I've heard, unofficially, that you'll get your bursary, so your travel costs will not be a problem, but I think you should stay put to do your research on Pax Romana.'

'Yes, of course,' she says, not revealing that she's already made a good start on this.

But there's only so much reading that can be undertaken on this unique period of Roman history before the one hundred years of peace across the Empire starts to become a bit tedious, and after several more days working in the college library, she can't bear the thought of taking more reading back to her temporary home in the B&B hotel. Neither does she want yet another walk in Kelvingrove Park, wonderful though it is. So, in search of distraction, she makes the mistake of trying to resume the life of an undergraduate; going for a night out in the student pubs. She doesn't come across anyone she knows, as she hoped she might, and she soon discovers the exclusiveness of well-formed student groups. And she's soon conscious that she's part of the diaspora of last year's graduates.

Fortunately, the next day she gets a text from Professor Dinsdale's secretary to say the scroll she left with the company has been read and they'll be happy to do the same with the other four. Jeannie telephones the company and finds that Mr X is out for the day, so she hurries to deliver the remaining scrolls. She's disappointed to find that the printout of the scroll they've read isn't available for collection and on her return to Glasgow she finds it difficult to settle, so she decides to go home for the next few days.

It seems that the events of the last week or so – and possibly reading about how Pax Romana affected everyday lives – has changed her perspective on her parents. On the train home she thinks she'll be able to relate to them as if she were an observer, rather than as the daughter who's irritated by their foibles. She brings to mind their television viewing habits; her mother's is a staple diet of the soaps and soft crime whodunnits, such as *Inspector Poirot*, whilst her father likes to watch each and every news bulletin and grumble his way through it. So, back home with her parents, Jeannie thinks she'll be able to cope with them as a cultural phenomenon.

For a couple of evenings she sits with them whilst they're watching television. She tries to read about some of the more obscure aspects of Pax Romana whilst taking in what going on, but she finds herself frequently glancing at the television, and discovers how easy it is to get hooked on the soaps. Seeing the danger of falling into a television torpor, she retreats to her bedroom.

The next day she returns to Glasgow. In college she offers to help tutor the first-year students who are in the middle of practical assignments in the large teaching lab. This is accepted, and in doing this voluntary work she finds both the company she needs and the pleasure of doing something useful. There's also the possibility of going out for a drink with another postgraduate student who's come up from Oxford, but Jeannie decides to avoid this.

It's a week and a half after her last visit to Mr X's company that another message comes via Professor Dinsdale's secretary. This time it's to tell her that all the scrolls have been read and Mr X will be in Glasgow in two days' time, and he'd like to meet Jeannie for lunch in what she knows is one of Glasgow's premier hotels, where he'll present her with the scrolls and their printouts.

Jeannie gives a lot of thought to what to wear for this important lunch-date. She has the occasional impulse to turn up in jeans and sweater, with tousled hair, to make it clear that she's not interested. But she knows this will make her look ridiculous in one of the city's best known hotel-restaurants. The fact is that she doesn't possess a set of clothes that are anywhere near suitable for the occasion, and she makes a quick visit home to see if she can borrow something of her mother's.

There's a section of her mother's more than ample wardrobe which contains the unworn garments Jeannie witnessed her mother purchase in John Lewis, in what she now understands to be her mother's way of maintaining her sense of contact with her father's much younger, late brother. Here, Jeannie finds a trouser suit. It's not remotely something she would have bought for herself, but it fits as if it was made for her. Moreover, and somewhat bizarrely, when she sees herself in the full-length mirror she feels completely safe; it's like she's behind a mask, anonymous, and she can do or say whatever she pleases.

Mr X opens their conversation by asking what she'd like to drink. She asks for sparkling water. He says, 'But this is a celebration! Wouldn't you like champagne?' She declines, and he suggests something less ostentatious, something Italian, to go with the successful scroll reading: 'Something like, say, Prosecco.'

She relents, saying, 'Just a glass then. But also sparkling water, please.'

'Of course,' he says. Then he suggests they go straight into the light main menu, saying that he's not one for large lunches. As he orders for them both, she again notices his wedding ring. For a moment she feels inhibited about saying anything about it, as if her real self might step out from behind the mask, but then she says, 'That's a very nice ring.'

'Yes, thank you,' he says.

She's surprised by this, by his not being in the slightest disconcerted by her recognising that he's married. Then she realises she's made the same mistake as she did with Giorgio, her remark suggesting that his involvement with someone else – in this case his wife – was not a problem. She's a little annoyed with herself for this early error, but still feels safe in the trouser suit she's wearing and she's confident that she'll be able to deal with what's happening so long as they remain in a public space. So when he asks what she's been doing since he last saw her, she sees the opportunity to gain lost ground. She chats about the voluntary work she's been doing with the archaeology students here in Glasgow, saying a teaching job in university might well suit her. Then she decides to give him a short talk on some aspects of Roman history.

She explains that since she met him, she's spent a lot of her time reading contemporary Roman history – contemporary to the writing of the scrolls, that is. She tells him that in many respects Roman society at the time, during the long period of peace known as Pax Romana, was very similar to our own. She outlines how slaves did every conceivable job: estate managers, secretaries, teachers, artisans and public servants. And like today's wage slaves, she says, they were paid and could build up a fund – a peculium – to buy their freedom. 'From there on the sky was the limit, except that entry to the uppermost rank of society, the nobility, was impossible in just one generation.'

Here Jeannie pauses. He's stopped eating, she's not yet started, so she eats a little of the excellent-looking lunch so as to catch up. But, fearing he might try to change the subject, she doesn't eat for too long before resuming where she was going.

'Another parallel between now and then is phallocentricity – the symbolic and actual fascination of the male with his penis,' she tells him. 'The difference is that now this is concealed behind a general interest in sex, whereas the Roman view of sex was graphic and explicit, particularly so concerning the phallus. Wall paintings in some of the most respectable houses in Herculaneum, for example, show couples in congress, occasionally with the assistance of their slaves. But it's the phallus itself that is most frequently depicted, or sculptured: phalluses painted over shop doorways, oil lamps made in the phallus shape, phalluses carved in the pavement, even phalluses used as street signs, pointing the direction. The phallus,' she concludes, 'is a symbol of male dominance – its most obvious message being that sexual penetration equates to power and pleasure.'

Jeannie now tucks into her really good lunch, looking up at him occasionally to gauge his reaction. When she catches his eye he smiles but says nothing. She thinks she might have got the better of him, but she's not absolutely certain of this and gives him a further moment to comment – or to change the subject.

But he does neither, so she adds: 'Of course, there's another aspect to the present day concealed display of phallus, and that's to do with male anxiety about manliness. Of not being a real man unless you're putting it about, of not being the real deal unless you're engaged in sexual conquests.'

She stops talking altogether at this point. She eats and holds him in her gaze. He smiles once, briefly, but seems unable to look her fully in the face until he decides to speak.

'I envy you your work, it must give you lots of interesting things to talk about. Regrettably, there's nothing I can say about mine.'

'But you've got a life apart from work, surely?' she says.

'Yes,' he says, 'But you don't want to hear about that.'

'Why not?'

'Well, it's the usual sort of things.'

'Like?'

'Oh, I don't know, like sailing a dinghy.'

From the moment he says this a fake smile reveals the mistake he knows he's just made. Mentioning sailing his dinghy has brought to mind the people he sails with: his friends, his wife perhaps and possibly his children. He's now open to question about them, no longer the lone wolf who set up this meeting. In seeing this, Jeannie is convinced that what he hoped to get from the lunch date is now seriously holed below the water.

Seeing that he's putting on a brave face, she asks no further questions.

He finishes his lunch before she does, and he's already moving on to thinking about the next course, asking if she'd like dessert. She says not, and he says, 'Well, in that case I won't either.'

He smiles, pleased, it seems, that they've agreed about something. Then, as the waiter clears their plates and asks if they'd like to see the dessert menu, or order coffee, Mr X steps in to suggest they take coffee in his room, adding, 'It will be more comfortable there.'

She's surprised by this, more so because it's said in front of the waiter, and she sees it as a last bid from a man who can't quite believe that his well-fashioned formula of seduction isn't working. So, she says she's happy to just finish her water.

The waiter bows tactfully and retreats.

Mr X now seems stuck for words and there's a moment when Jeannie actually feels sorry for him. But the part of her where such sympathy lives is overshadowed by impatience. 'You did bring the scrolls with you, didn't you? They're in your room here in the hotel, I take it?'

'Yes,' he says, suddenly brightening, looking like he thinks she may have only been teasing, and soon they'll be on their way to his room. But Jeannie quickly dashes any hope of this. 'In that case would you mind getting the scrolls, please?'

'Of course, of course,' he says, as if delivering the scrolls to her at table had always been his intention.

Immediately he's out of sight Jeannie is concerned that she's overplayed her hand. And she's very much on edge during the next five minutes when he doesn't make an appearance. But then the waiter comes over carrying the ribbed aluminium container. 'Reception asked me to bring this to you,' he says as he reaches her table. 'It's from the gentleman who just checked out.'

The waiter then glances through the window. Jeannie follows his line of sight, and sure enough there's Mr X walking hurriedly towards the railway station, pulling a small black, wheeled case behind him. She is all fingers and thumbs as she quickly tries to open the small aluminium case, imagining that he might have removed the scrolls to spite her. But no, the scrolls are where they should be, and each is wrapped neatly in its own paper printout. She now thinks she should rush after him to say thank you, and perhaps apologise for giving him the wrong impression at their first meeting. But the waiter is hovering, and she asks if she can be moved to another table.

Her wish to be moved to the other side of the restaurant is pure impulse. But when she's made the move, she understands her motivation: to remove herself from Mr X's sphere of attention. In seeing this another thought comes to mind. Perhaps he's left her to pay the lunch bill. It's possible that the attentive waiter has read her thoughts, for at that very moment he says, 'The bill is settled, would madam now like some coffee?'

'Yes,' she says. 'Yes, I would, and can you tell me what time the restaurant closes?'

'It stays open all day, till late,' he says, adding, 'There is no hurry.'

He backs away, forcing a smile whilst tilting his head slightly towards her, as if to say, 'No problem, madam, this is how it sometimes happens.'

With coffee on the table, and the best part of half a bottle of Prosecco on ice, Jeannie begins her work on the scroll printouts.

The first thing she wants to know, the thing that's really important, is does Rufus Mettius's writing live up to expectation? To answer this, she quickly skims through each of the printouts to get the gist of what's in each scroll. And the thing that stands out for her from this reading is Rufus Mettius saying what he'd do if he became a freeman: he'd go to Naples where he'd gain his place 'on the citizens list'. Then he'd go on to '...somewhere much greater...' Jeannie understands him to mean he'd go on to Rome, and she finds this reassuring. In her imagination she now sees him escaping Asinius' clutches, then on his way to Naples before the first of the pyroclastic waves rolls over the villa killing everything that's still living, even those sheltering from the earlier downfalls of ash and pumice. She sees Rufus Mettius as part of a straggling crowd heading towards Naples. She can see that in such chaos a runaway slave won't be noticed, and, with a skill-set such as his, he'll have no difficulty in finding employment in Naples. And she's optimistic that if he made it to Rome there's a chance she might yet find him.

By mid-afternoon, still in the hotel restaurant, Jeannie has a fully worked-out plan of action. She'll make four copies of each of the five scroll printouts. One will be lodged with the archaeology department here in Glasgow, another for Angus, the third for the conservation department in Naples, together with Rufus Mettius's undamaged scrolls, and the fourth copy will be for her to work on. The original printout of the scrolls, which for her equates with the scrolls themselves, she'll keep in the brown paper parcel under her bed. As for a timetable, she's worked that out as well. She'll give up her room at the B&B hotel and, to save money, stay with her parents whilst she makes a translation of all five scrolls. What with her mother's voluntary work in the charity shop, and her father out at work all day, and her staying in her room, she'll have a good deal of time to press on with her work. She'll give herself exactly one week to complete the task, and she'll book the early flight to Naples for the day after this deadline.

Chapter 5

Investigations

Jeannie finds Angus in the site office. After a brief exchange of formalities, she tries to deliver the speech she's rehearsed on the flight over, explaining that the electronic reading of the scrolls was done as a one-off favour and that's why no further scrolls can be read in Scotland. But she's only able to make a start on the speech before Angus waves aside what she's saying.

'No problem, no problem!' he tells her. 'Dinsdale rang yesterday. He explained the situation. The important thing is that you've established that electronic reading of the scrolls is possible, so why not here in Italy? Listen, I've got an appointment with the Director of Excavations this afternoon, we're going to sort out approaching an Italian electronics company with this in mind, and he's going to see if they'd like to be sponsors of the new museum.' He beams. 'It's to be a prestigious project.'

'That's great,' she says, feeling greatly relieved.

'Which bit is great?' says Angus with another broad smile.

'Which bit? Well, all of it – looking for sponsorship for the project and having the rest of the scrolls read here in Italy.'

'You've missed something,' he says with an even bigger smile.

'What's that?'

'The new museum – approval's come through at last!'

Angus throws up his arms in joy, and for a moment Jeannie thinks he's doing a jig as he turns around several times, the index fingers of each hand pointing in every direction. But it turns out he's looking for the architect's drawings he's put down somewhere, pointing to the various places where he might have left them. When he sees the drawings, he snatches them up and leading the way from the site office says, 'Come on, Jeannie!'

They stop by the improvised bench-seat made by the Three Girls of Naples, overlooking the site. 'Look,' he says, pointing to the architect's drawing, 'the whole villa will be restored to its former glory, except for the scriptorium. See, there's to be an ultra-modern glass structure sweeping over it, and the scriptorium is to be preserved in its excavated state, to show and celebrate the work of the archaeologists.'

After this Angus is silent for perhaps a whole half-minute, simply looking from the architect's drawing to the excavation site, imagining, it seems, what the restored villa, with its sweep of glass over the scriptorium, will look like. Then, reverting to something more like the usual Angus, he tells her that with the last of this year's student gone the hostel has closed for the winter. The few things she'd left in her room are in a box in the site office.

'The good news is that you've got sole use of the flat the museum service owns in Naples. And the rail pass we keep in the site office is yours for the winter,' he adds.

For a short while Jeannie is speechless. Then, when she's asked where the flat is, and been told it's on the edge of the old city, Angus suggests she might like to spend the rest of the day moving in. Again, she's silent, hardly able to believe her good fortune as Angus turns from her to go back to the site office.

When she joins him, Angus is again at his desk, poring over what looks like a list he's preparing. He doesn't look up, and Jeannie takes the opportunity to put the aluminium case and the folder she's been carrying on the corner of his desk.

'What are these?' he says when he finally sees them.

'The scrolls are in the case with a paper copy of their texts, together with a printout of my translations. I'm assuming they'll go to the conservation department. The folder has your paper copy of the scrolls and my translations. What I can tell you from reading the scrolls is that the name of the slave-scribe who wrote them is Rufus Mettius Diomedes and his master, presumably the villa owner, is called Asinius. If we put what Rufus Mettius has to say in his scrolls together with the drafts we've got here in the scroll workshop, we have a pretty complete picture of life at the villa.'

Having gained Angus's full attention, she adds, 'And Rufus Mettius's scrolls are what I plan to focus my research on.'

Angus may have heard all this and understood it completely, but he homes in on just one thing: 'So you've got names for both the scribe and his master?'

It's annoying that, yet again, Angus seems uninterested in her research, but given that the villa is to be restored as a museum Jeannie recognises that the names of its occupants are the more important matter, and adds, 'We also have names for two of the other slaves in the household. Both females.'

'That's excellent. So the scribe's scrolls have already proved their worth.'

'Yes, I think so.'

For a moment Jeannie hopes this acknowledgement of the worth of the scrolls will bring Angus back to the matter of her research, but no:

'So, we only have the one name for Asinius?'

'Yes.'

'Well, it's a start. We're of the view that the body cavity we found is, in fact, the villa's high-status owner, so we'll call his plaster-cast Asinius from now on.'

'Have any other body cavities been found?' Jeannie asks, now concerned that they might have found Rufus Mettius in her absence.

'No, and it doesn't look likely there are any – we're down to floor level in all the rooms'

'Good,' she says, relieved.

'Good?' Angus questions, adding, 'Ideally we'd have found a body cavity in every room, if the museum's to attract much in the way of public interest.'

'Yes, of course,' she says, 'I wasn't thinking.'

This mild rebuke brings Jeannie's hopes of discussing her research to an end, but the conversation is to take yet another turn.

'Anyway, where we're at is this. We've almost cleared every room. All the artefacts, the oil lamps and so on, have gone to the conservation department for cleaning. We've got a photographic record of where we found the carbonised tables, chairs and beds and so on and they'll be replaced with reproductions exactly where we found them. Giorgio and I are still working on the scriptorium and we're hoping the wall mural restoration team will be able to make a start straight after Christmas.'

'A lot's been achieved then, whilst I've been away,' Jeannie says, feeling humbled by the enormous amount of work that must have been done in her absence.

'Yes, and there's still a way to go. I'd like you to spend some time on site, but what I want you to do now, now we know the villa's going to be a museum, is to work on the guidebook. The publicity department want to call it something like Daily Life at the Villa and its People. The scribe's scrolls – Rufus Mettius Diomedes, didn't you call him – sound like they'll be really useful for this purpose.'

That Angus has said nothing about her research now does not matter, for Jeannie instantly grasps that any work she does on Rufus Mettius's scrolls for the guidebook will lay the foundations of her research. She touches the folder she's put on his desk, saying, 'I think you'll find Rufus Mettius's scrolls interesting.'

Angus does not appear to have been listening, until he says, 'Ah, yes, Professor Dinsdale said the same. I'll read them at the weekend.'

She moves to Naples that afternoon. The flat is quite spacious and well furnished. It's on the third floor of a substantial apartment block, but because it's at the back of the building, on the shaded side, it has the feel of a place you wouldn't choose to spend too much time in. It's used by the museum service for newly appointed staff moving into the city, as temporary accommodation until they find a place of their own. For budgetary reasons the museum service won't be recruiting any new staff for quite a while, so Jeannie has the place for the foreseeable future.

On her first Saturday as a resident of Naples Jeannie returns to the routine she'd adopted when on her own in Glasgow during the long summer vacation. That is, she decides to get to know the city as a tourist. By mid-afternoon she's in one of Naples' oldest districts, Quartieri Spagnoli, and she recognises the street where Rosa lives. She's curious to know what's happened to Rosa, and although she has a clear recollection of being sharp with her – letting her know in no uncertain terms that her mother needs to know that she's a woman – she hopes she'll have been forgiven, since the remark was well intentioned. So there's a degree of hesitation before Jeannie presses the intercom button at the communal entrance of Rosa's mother's apartment. And there's a second reason for this slight delay, which is that Jeannie recalls Rosa's mother's incessant talking. On this occasion, however, she reassures herself with the thought that as an uninvited guest she'll be able to uninvite herself if and when she pleases.

Rosa answers the intercom with a single 'Si.'

Jeannie announces herself, in Italian, as 'Jeannie from the scavi.'

After a moment the electronic lock on the communal door click-clacks to let Jeannie know it's open, then, through the intercom, Rosa asks her to come up. She's waiting outside the door of her mother's apartment, but it's not to greet Jeannie as a friend. No, Rosa neither offers her cheek nor puts out her hand, but in an unfamiliarly quiet voice says, 'Things have changed.'

She looks pale and dark beneath the eyes. For a little while she seems reluctant to say anything and Jeannie imagines she's about to be told that Rosa's mother is unwell – or even dead.

When Rosa does eventually speak, it's to announce that Alfredo's here.

They go into the apartment, Rosa leading her to the kitchen, saying she was just making coffee, and would Jeannie like to join them? This said in a hushed voice, sufficient to make Jeannie think that it might be Alfredo who's unwell. Perhaps he's got a terrible headache. But the television in the lounge can be heard, so this seems unlikely.

Jeannie watches Rosa as she makes the coffee, trying to fathom out what's going on. Then, when Rosa comes to put the coffee cups on a tray, Jeannie notices a gold ring on her third finger. Her first thought is that Rosa's got engaged, but a second sight of the gold band suggests she is already married. Jeannie is so surprised by this that she misses the opportunity to ask if congratulations are in order before Rosa leads the way into the sitting room. Her mother is moving a small coffee table close to the rangy legs of a lightly bearded man sitting in front of the television.

'Mama, you know Jeannie from the scavi,' she says in Italian.

Her mother smiles, but only briefly, before taking a cup of coffee from the tray Rosa is holding and putting it on the small table beside Alfredo, asking if he'd like milk.

'Si, grazie,' he says, without taking his eyes from the television.

'Alfredo, this is Jeannie,' Rosa says in English, this time in a much firmer voice. 'She was my supervisor at the excavation.'

'Si si,' he says, adding, 'Hi, Jeannie.'

He glances at the television before telling her in good clear

English, 'It is Manchester United playing Chelsea.' This, it seems, is his explanation for why he won't be giving Jeannie any more attention.

The three women sit on the settee, their knees pointing to the small coffee table before them. Jeannie and Rosa are side by side, with Rosa's mother nearest to Alfredo. This arrangement of furniture and people appears to sum up what's going on here and Jeannie wonders if the dark rings under Rosa's eyes are a sign of morning sickness: perhaps her earlier suggestion that Rosa's mother needed recognise her as a woman, and Rosa giving herself to Alfredo, have happened in quick succession.

In the stilted conversation that follows, repeatedly held up by Rosa's mother's requests for translation, Jeannie tries to glean what's actually happened. Rosa, however, keeps taking the conversation back to what Jeannie's been doing since she last saw her. And, of course, there's a lot to tell her, what with Jeannie's trip back to Scotland, and Rufus Mettius's scrolls being read, and the excavation moving on apace, to say nothing of her moving into Naples. So, by the time they've finished their coffee, and Jeannie needs to use the loo, she's no further forward in finding out what's going on here.

Returning from the toilet and seeing the door of Rosa's room slightly ajar, Jeannie can't help but pause for a moment. The twin beds have been pushed together, each still with its own single duvet, one of which has been straightened whilst the other is still rumpled. This narrowly upright view into the room suggests just one thing: Rosa is already unhappy with her marriage. Jeannie takes this thought to the sitting room, where Alfredo is now alone.

Then she takes it to the kitchen, where Rosa and her mother are washing up the coffee cups. Several times Rosa stops what she's doing, and, as she turns to face Jeannie, she covers her ring finger.

Soon after this Jeannie makes her excuse to leave, but before she goes she suggests they meet up one evening. Jeannie writes the telephone number and address of her flat on a scrap of paper and puts it on the table.

Rosa looks unsure as to whether she'll take it.

The effect of this visit is to make Jeannie abandon tourism for the day and head back to the flat in order to get on with her work on Rufus Mettius's scrolls. As the city bus trundles across Naples, making its many jerky stops, Jeannie is shaken into the realisation of where her impulse to get on with this work has come from. She found the way Alfredo was being indulged quite shocking, particularly as there was nothing to suggest it was what he demanded, but rather what the two women – and in particular Rosa's mother – had pressed on him. And it's this that makes her think that in her own way she's being unduly deferential towards her imagined Roman. She's been shilly-shallying, putting off getting started on her work on the scrolls because she's in awe of Rufus Mettius. On realising this, her impulse becomes one of resolve. Yes, she'll make a start on the scrolls this evening, and what she'll do from the very start is to put what Rufus Mettius has to say into context so that what he says will make complete sense to the modern reader.

Back at the apartment, fully resolved, she sets up her study area at the table in the living room. This is quickly done, her resources being her laptop, her translations of the scrolls and a notepad of unlined A4 paper. She keys in 'Pax Romana' on her laptop to access the notes she made in the college library. Then she takes the notepad and makes a handwritten copy of the opening sentence of Rufus Mettius' first scroll:

I am Rufus Mettius Diomedes, slave-scribe to Asinius who in every way is a useless creature.

In writing out just this one sentence in longhand Jeannie regains the intense sense of contact she had with Rufus Mettius whilst translating his scrolls in her bedroom back in Scotland. It's a feeling of intimacy so alluring that she's tempted to go on copying out his words. But her resolve to do justice to the opening sentence, to contextualise all that it says and implies, kicks in, and she makes a start on what the scroll seems to ask of her:

This statement made by a slave about his master may seem surprising, since we do not usually think of slaves as literate. In fact, during the long period of peace in the Roman Empire – the Pax Romana – it often happened that vernae (slaves born to existing household slaves) received a good education so that they might carry out duties, which might include such things as tutoring the master's children, or even running the family business. What is probably less surprising to us is that a slave might harbour hostile feelings towards his or her owner, especially if the slave were mistreated. In fact, in this case here there is no evidence of mistreatment. Quite the opposite, for according to Rufus Mettius he lives much the same day-to-day life as Asinius. In the villa, they eat the same food, and the room where Rufus Mettius sleeps, and usually works, is not cramped and only slightly smaller than his master's. So, the hostility towards Asinius, or more accurately the criticism of him, does not stem from physical maltreatment.

Another cause of resentment, anger or frustration, for any slave during this period is the possibility that however well he or she serves their master there is no prospect of their being freed. Certainly, this is true of Rufus Mettius, who several times in his scrolls speaks of his ambition to be 'put on the citizen's list'. But the possibility of never being free is not the main grudge that comes across in reading Rufus Mettius's five scrolls, rather it is to do with his master's unwillingness and inability to use his own time, his learning, or his considerable wealth, for the benefit of anyone but himself. To fully appreciate the nature of the complaint Rufus Mettius has against Asinius we need to look at the wider culture.

Much, if not most, of Roman culture at this time was derived from the Greeks. The architecture and the widespread use of statues in public places are perhaps the two most obvious examples. Also, Greek was the language of first choice in ennobled circles, and no educated Roman would consider himself a man of consequence unless he could quote Ancient Greek writers like Homer, Herodotus or Thucydides. But it is the adoption of Greek philosophy, its distortion and dilution, which perhaps tells us most about the Romans of this period.

Two very different Greek schools of philosophy had widespread following in the Roman world at this time: that of the Stoics and the Epicureans, of which Asinius declares himself a member. The founder of Epicureanism was Aristippus, whose conviction was that the aim of life is to attain the highest possible sensory enjoyment and avoid pain in all its forms. This idea was later developed by Epicurus, who emphasised that the pleasurable results of an action must always be weighed against its consequences. Also, he thought that pleasure was more than just sensual delight and extended into such things as the appreciation of friendship and art. But such concerns for the consequence of action, and the appreciation of friendship, did not go beyond the immediate circle of fellow Epicureans, who advocated seclusion from wider society. By Asinius' time, nearly four centuries later, Epicureanism was little more than a high-minded rationale for the self-indulgence of the privileged and wealthy. In contrast, Stoicism, at the same time, was the philosophy of community engagement: of politics, notably of those who wished for the return of the Republic and their participation in its government – not forgetting the desire for their own self-advancement.

The fundamental belief of the Stoics was that we are all part of a world ruled by universal law. Each individual person is a miniature version, or 'microcosmos', reflecting the natural law of the larger world: the 'macrocosmos.' So natural law governs all mankind, and in this sense all are equal – even slaves. It should not be assumed, however, that the much-improved conditions of slaves at the time of Rufus Mettius was brought about by the application of Stoicism, rather that, like Epicureanism, this philosophy provided a rationale for what was already happening. In fact, as historians writing about this period often point out, the one thing most responsible for the improved condition of slaves at this time was that the supply of slaves through conquest, or the subjugation of tribes within the Empire, had dried up. Over the previous one hundred years there had been a period of peace – the Pax Romana – and an increasing reliance on home-bred slaves. Having invested in their rearing and training, and in their becoming more like members of the family, it was not in the owners' interests to treat their slaves harshly. Stoics such as Seneca encouraged the idea of a duty of kindness to slaves, but it looks likely that he was voicing a changed attitude rather than bringing it about.

Jeannie stops writing at this point. She feels she's said everything she needs to in order to put Rufus Mettius's opening statement fully into context. But in writing about the effect of Pax Romana on the lives of slaves such as Rufus Mettius she's lost the intimacy she felt with him when writing out in longhand just one sentence of his actual words. She's tempted to try to regain this feeling of contact with him by writing out the next passage of the scroll, and in this way bring Rufus Mettius back into her living presence, but there's also a sense within her that says she should resist this. It's the feeling that she needs to hold off making an emotional commitment to Rufus Mettius until she knows for sure that he survived the eruption.

Early to bed, she makes more plans. At the site meeting, first thing on Monday, she will, of course, show a willingness to do whatever is asked of her to help complete the excavation. She'll also ask Angus if he's had a chance to read Rufus Mettius' scrolls over the weekend. If he has, she'll suggest that one of the things the visitors to the villa museum might be interested in is what happened to him. She'll mention the possibility that if he escaped the pyroclastic blast and made his way to Naples to obtain work and his citizenship, and then go on to Rome to fulfil his ambition to take a place in the Senate, then perhaps a trace of him might be found there.

Having decided this, sleep comes easily to her.

Jeannie is the first person on site on Monday morning and she goes to the scroll workshop to leave her bag and find a particular scroll which has alterations made in Asinius' hand. The scroll she's after describes how Asinius says it's only the likes of him, the Epicurians, who can appreciate fine wine. It's a scroll Rufus Mettius refers to, saying how the household slaves have wine tasting sessions of their own, after Asinius's dinner parties.

When she's found the scroll she's looking for she puts it to one side, then she goes over to the excavation. She finds Angus at work in the scriptorium. It's the first time she's been there since she came back from Scotland. At a glance, the enormous progress that's been made is obvious. And Angus seems genuinely pleased to see her.

'So,' he says triumphantly, 'we now have the full picture!'

He then describes what's been revealed in Jeannie's absence.

'The villa is a half-way-house, a stepping-stone between the events at Pompeii and Herculaneum, showing some of the features of each,' he tells her, pointing to different parts of the room as he explains the course of events.

'First, the earth tremors caused some damage, but no serious collapse, though parts of the roof structure must have been opened up with tiles falling onto the mosaic. Then the eruption itself, with a relatively light fall of ash and pumice descending on the villa in its early stage. Next, the first of the pyroclastic waves, killing anyone remaining in the villa but leaving clothes and leather intact, as is the case with Asinius here. Then the much heavier fall of ash and pumice making its way into the house through open doors, windows and the damaged roof. This filled the scriptorium to a depth of about two feet, completely entombing Asinius. Then the second pyroclastic wave, so hot it carbonised anything made of wood and not already covered by the ash and pumice, burning people and animals to the bone. Finally, the huge fall of volcanic debris covering the whole area to a depth of up to twenty feet.'

When Angus has finished describing the course of the eruption he's silent for a moment, looking around him, admiring his achievement. It's a moment that lasts a little too long for Jeannie's comfort in that it provokes a prick of conscience about her hanging on to Rufus Mettius' carbonised tablet, where he says it was he who killed Asinius.

'Right,' says Angus, getting to his feet, 'time to get ready for the meeting.'

She waits until he's left the roofless scriptorium, then goes over to the plaster cast of Asinius. It's the first time she's seen the cast exposed and she's impressed by the detail preserved on the surface. And, yes, sure enough, she can see there's a swelling behind the left ear. Such a swelling of soft tissue could only have occurred if Asinius had lived for some hours after he was injured. If Rufus Mettius had caused this injury, he would have had as little as four or five hours to make his escape. It would have been a close-run thing, and she imagines the events as they unfolded. Asinius is clutching one of his precious scrolls to his chest, while with the other hand he's hanging on to Rufus Mettius to keep him from leaving. There's the terror of what's going on around them, all the other slaves having already fled. To save himself, Rufus Mettius reaches for something to fend off Asinius. Imagining this, Jeannie looks for what Rufus Mettius might have reached for, but the room is denuded of its artefacts, as they have all been sent to Naples for cleaning and restoration.

In stepping back from Asinius's cast, giving up on finding what he might have been struck with, she notices a small niche at eye-level beside the many much larger niches which once held Asinius's collection of scrolls. This niche has only been partially cleared of solidified ash and pumice and it looks like another example of Angus showing the work of the archaeologist to the public. In the niche there's an almost fully excavated bronze statue of Hercules holding up the world. It fits closely to the top of the niche and it's awkward for Jeannie to get her hand around it, but with the thumb of her right hand pointing upwards she's able to take a firm hold of Hercules's torso. With this grip she feels sure she's holding this small but heavy object exactly as Rufus Mettius would have.

It's a strange feeling. It's as if nearly two thousand years has been bridged in an instant, for she feels sure Rufus Mettius would have held the statue exactly as she is now.

Making her way to the team meeting, and almost at the door of the site office, she's suddenly halted by a thought: why, when his life was in such danger, did Rufus Mettius take the time and trouble to write what he did on the tablet and carefully place it amongst his five scrolls, if not to make a statement? But a statement about what?

She'd like to give this some serious thought, but in opening the door of the site office she can see that Angus and Giorgio, together with the elderly twin volunteers, are waiting. She apologises for her lateness as they all look in her direction.

Angus is uncharacteristically pleasant when he says she is in fact early, by two minutes. He spends a little time outlining what he'd like done during the week, then he generously praises Jeannie for the interest she's taken in the slave-scribe's scrolls, saying that otherwise they might have been overlooked. 'What's more,' he says, 'they've been electronically read – showing that it can be done!' He adds that this hopefully means that all the other scrolls can also be read without being unpicked. Having said this, Angus hands out a copy of Jeannie's translation of the scrolls to Giorgio and the twin volunteers, remarking on how they make such interesting reading. To underscore this, he says: 'I've asked Jeannie to make the scrolls the basis of the guidebook to the villa, and she's agreed to do this.'

Giorgio and the elderly twins, Gino and Gillo, nod their approval.

Jeannie seizes her moment. 'I think it would be of great interest to visitors to the villa museum if they could be told what happened to the slave-scribe, Rufus Mettius,' she tells the meeting. 'In the scrolls he speaks of his ambition to achieve his freedom and citizenship in Naples, then go on to Rome and the Senate. If he made it there, it's possible we might trace him.'

'Tracking him down is something I'll raise with the Director of Excavations when I see him this afternoon,' Angus assures her.

The elderly twins nod their enthusiasm for Angus's proposal.

Jeannie's meets the Director of Excavations in his office two days later. All goes well, although at first she's distracted by the thought that she's already met him. She knows this is extremely unlikely, if not impossible, and it takes a little while for her to realises why this thought came to her, which is that he closely resembles the late Donald Sinden, an actor who would be unknown to her except that she's seen him in the movies her mother's so fond of watching on daytime television. It's because the director has Donald Sinden's manner of speaking – as if he's in a tunnel without the benefit of peripheral vision – that he does not notice Jeannie's little 'Aha!' when she realises why he looks so familiar.

The director continues, as if playing his part in a Sherlock Holmes movie:

'Ye-es,' he says with a slightly nasal drawl, 'yours is an interesting case to research. You'll of course be aware that in Herculaneum the citizens' lists were inscribed on marble plaques for public display. How they kept them up to date with citizens dying, and new names needing to be added, isn't entirely clear. But at the time of Vesuvius' eruption, Herculaneum had relatively few citizens, being more of a retreat for the wealthy with their many slaves. Naples was, and is, an altogether different proposition. Always busy and bustling, so citizens' lists would almost certainly have been kept on papyrus scrolls – if kept at all. And there's the rub – have any of those survived? I doubt it, but it's something we'll have to ask our archivists to look into. In our favour, it's quite a narrow time frame we're dealing with. You say our man, Rufus Mettius Diomedes, if he escaped the first of the pyroclastic waves, would have made his way to Naples and stayed long enough to establish his citizenship, then gone on to Rome, you believe.'

Here the director pauses, purses his lips and inhales deeply through flared nostrils.

'Ye-es. I rather think, from what you've said, that our man wouldn't have stayed more than a couple of years in Naples, and when he made his way to Rome he would have headed for the Senate. So, if he was in Rome, we've got two ways to track him down. One is to trawl through every document we have which mentions the Senate, and Senators, during this period. The other means at our disposal is the funerary inscriptions on stone tablets, and there are many thousands of those in Rome. So, it could be that we're looking for a needle in a haystack. The other problem I suspect we'll have is with his name. When slaves were officially freed they often took the name of their master. In this case we only have the one name, Asinius, to go on, and that's far from uncommon. But I rather think that as a runaway – which is what he was – he wouldn't have used his master's name. In the chaos that followed the eruption it's probable that runaway slaves were hardly noticed, especially if they were accomplished and could find high status work.'

Having walked these sentences around his office, the director stops to take a sip of the tea he's been carrying close to his chest. Then he adds:

'The name itself is interesting. Rufus and Mettius are Roman names but Diomedes suggests Greek lineage. And this fits well with what we know of the Greek-speaking literate slaves – invariably more intellectually capable than their masters – who originated in the easterly parts of the Empire.'

Having walked a few steps further, he stops again. Then, facing the seated Jeannie with a smile, the cup of tea close to his lips, he suggests: 'You should assume our man stuck to his own name.' He then tells her he thinks it's worth spending some time in Rome to see if she can track down his funerary plaque. The director does not, however, suggest how these visits, and this time in Rome, will be paid for.

Leaving his office, Jeannie feels greatly encouraged, even if not financially supported. The director has more or less confirmed her view that it was unlikely there would be a scroll record of Rufus Mettius' citizenship in Naples. The only way in which scrolls of this period were known to have survived, other than being carbonised, was by being preserved in places of extreme aridity – as was the case for the Dead Sea scrolls. She'll clearly need to check with the archivists in Naples as to whether there are any scroll records of this period, but she fully expects the result to be negative, and she'll soon be on her way to Rome.

First thing next day Jeannie finds Angus in the scriptorium. He's putting out the tools for Gino and Gillo to use. After a polite 'Good morning' she gets straight to the point: 'I saw the director yesterday and he was supportive of my spending some time in Rome to see if I can track down Rufus Mettius.'

'Yes, I know, he phoned,' says Angus. 'But he didn't say how it would be paid for.'

'No, he didn't tell me that either.'

Jeannie waits for Angus to respond, but he seems distracted

by what he's doing. So, she adds, 'Perhaps I could use some of my travel grant?'

'Yes, you'll need to do that if you want to stay over in Rome. The best I can do is provide a month-long rail pass.'

Perhaps it's the unenthusiastic way in which Angus has offered her the rail pass that makes the offer sound ungenerous. But when Jeannie realises that a month-long rail pass will be more than sufficient, she has the impulse to hug him. It's possible that Angus has seen this coming, for he moves a little way from her. And in seeing this, seeing that he does not want such physical contact, things fall into place. The waiter at Angus's favourite restaurant in Naples is, of course, his boyfriend. And yes, there was that strange kind of stiffness in Angus's posture when Simply Elaine touched him lightly on the arm.

Having obtained the timetable for the trains to Rome, Jeannie works out the schedule for her research. She'll do day trips, using her time on the train to work on her laptop and search for any records she can find of the Senate at this time. She'll also do a couple of stopovers so that she can arrange both morning and afternoon meetings with the various archivists and curators in the city's museum service. On these stop-over visits she'll also have a look at various sites of interest – sites Rufus Mettius would have known.

This, she tells herself, is to assimilate a sense of his life in Rome.

On the first of these stop-overs, and it's almost dusk, Jeannie finds herself lingering by a bridge, the Ponte Fabricio, said to have been virtually untouched since it was built in 62 BC and therefore unchanged more than a hundred years later when Rufus Mettius might have crossed it. She tries to imagine him on the bridge, and, if he would just turn to face her, she thinks she might know exactly what he looks like.

But he refuses.

Returning to Naples that evening, and almost at her apartment block, she thinks she sees Rosa leaving the building. Jeannie hurries after and calls to her. Rosa stops and turns. She looks pale and dark around the eyes – though this could be the effect of the streetlight. Jeannie gives her a hug and asks her to come up to the flat. It's nice and warm inside and Jeannie invites Rosa to take her coat off, and to have a seat whilst she makes coffee. Rosa is disinclined to do this, seeming very unsettled, and she waits in the doorway of the kitchen whilst Jeannie prepares the coffee. Jeannie asks how she is, but she puts off asking how things are with her mother, and with Alfredo, guessing that one or the other is the reason for the visit.

Jeannie does not have long to wait, Rosa clearly wanting to get something off her chest.

'Jeannie,' she says, before the coffee percolator has even started to bump, 'We have been married for two months and I have not enjoyed sex once.'

Having observed Rosa with her mother, and her mother with Alfredo, Jeannie is not at all surprised to hear this. She herself had felt inhibited by her mother, and the all-too familiar people in her own small town, and it wasn't until she could get away from all of them when she went to university that she felt she could be herself. So, what Rosa has just told her connects directly to her own experience.

'Have you only slept with Alfredo in your mother's apartment?'

'Yes, there only,' says Rosa, already brightening, understanding that Jeannie is on the same wavelength. Then Rosa adds, 'Do you think it makes a difference?'

'Yes,' says Jeannie, 'all the difference in the world.'

'You think I should go to stay with him in Perugia?'

'Yes.'

'But Alfredo only has a tiny room, what you call a "bed-sit", and he is embarrassed just to talk about it.'

'That won't matter.'

'You think I should go.'

'Yes, you must.'

'I should tell my mother?'

'Phone her when you're on the train – tell her where you're going. Tell Alfredo the same. And if he doesn't pick up, leave a message to say you're on your way.'

'You really think so?'

'Yes. Do you have the money for the fare?'

'Yes, enough to get there.'

'Then go, Rosa. Go.'

There's half a moment's hesitation before Rosa buttons up her coat, leaving the coffee Jeannie's just poured untouched.

As on the previous occasion when she saw Rosa, when Alfredo was being fussed over by her mother, the effect of this is on Jeannie is to bring to mind thoughts about how she's relating to her Roman. This time, however, she chooses to resume her intimacy with Rufus Mettius by writing out a whole scroll in longhand.

I can now speak of what people call 'the love of their life', now it is over, and I think love a delusion.

Flavia came to the villa as a part of Asinius's inheritance from a rich uncle who had no legitimate children to pass his estate onto. She had been a domestic slave in the uncle's villa, and possibly his uncle's favourite. At the time of her arrival, I thought nothing of her past, smitten only by her beauty. From the first time we were able to talk together we became a pair, she wanting to know how I had come to be here. I told her how I had been given by another member of Asinius's family when at the same age as she was now, though with me it was to settle a debt. She put a hand on my arm and said, 'We are alike then.' When I told her I was the son of a slave girl and her master, she said she was such a daughter, and she put both hands on my arm saying, 'Then we are as one.'

So, I quickly and willingly became Flavia's protector, in so far as I was able.

The women in the household, the slaves, for there are no other women at the villa, share a practice. All keep a small, firm and evenly round sea sponge which they soak in vinegar, and the effectiveness of this can be attested by there having been only one child born in my time here. When the women are called upon to serve, they also soak the sponge in olive oil. Neither Asinius, nor the friends he entertains, have the ability or the inclination to bring them to excitement, and the oil saves them from discomfort.

Until Flavia's arrival I had paired with little Vibia, who then worked in the kitchen. Soon after my arrival, on the first occasion of meeting Vibia, she followed me into the atrium. When I stopped, she had me bend so she could tell me something. She cupped her hands about my ear and in a hot whisper told me she could visit me in the night as often as I pleased, and more often to suit her needs. This suited me until Flavia arrived.

I did not know the strength of Vibia's feelings for me, or that she had any, until then. She had always come to my room in the early part of the night, and it was always her desire to squat on me and not linger more than a moment. After Flavia's arrival Vibia stopped coming to my room, she gave me hostile looks and soon became pregnant by the roofer's son. I might have known nothing of this but for the remarks the roofer made. I will not repeat all his words but say only how he informed me that though I might have had Vibia, his son was man enough to 'knock her up'. For a while, that is until I made sure to stay out of his way, he never missed a chance to tell me that he and his son could come and go as they pleased, and Vibia was now a free woman. Free, I thought, to slave for his wife in the kitchen, but I did not say this.

His remark about how he could come and go as he pleased is not unusual for the men who come to do their work at the villa. It was the same with the plumber who came to fix the fountain, and the builder who extended the garden wall, and their attitude is not difficult to understand. They look around and see the women of the household, all neatly dressed and better fed than they are. It is clear to see, they think it is a good life here. They are envious of me, no doubt, and resentful of the life we have compared to what they can afford on their meagre earnings. So, what they say is a response to what they feel, and I do not rise to it but tell myself that in some ways bondage has its advantages. But what the roofer said about Vibia being pregnant touched a nerve.

Early on, in the times of intimacy with Flavia we would afterwards talk about how it might be if we were free and had a living. What we mostly talked about was of having our own children, and whether we would rather it was a boy or a girl to start with. It was a dream, of course, but one that could happen if I became a free man. Yet it was not a dream that could last.

When Asinius was entertaining, me in attendance with my clay tablets at the ready to take down his profound thoughts and quips, I noticed how Flavia tried to catch the eye of one of his guests. When this happened a second time, with the same guest some weeks later, I began to think about it more seriously. I had noticed that she used olive oil for our nights together, and, at the time, I simply thought this a practice she had brought with her. But now, with Flavia beneath me, her moaning seemed exaggerated and a poisonous thought began to seep through me. Soon Flavia was asking me to do it as I used to, and I was becoming jealous of the nights she spent with Asinius' fellow Epicurean, Septimius.

It was, as they say, 'a shock but not a surprise' when one afternoon I came back to my room to find a message on a freshly made clay tablet, written in the hand I had taught Flavia. 'I will always love you,' it said. Later in the day I learned from the eager tongues of the other women that she had been taken by Septimius, that she had hopes of marriage and the kind of freedom that comes with it.

At a distance of nearly two years it is not difficult to write about *this. I understand Flavia as I understand the builder, the roofer and the plumber, as I understand myself. We all make the best of what we have.*

The effect of writing out the scroll in longhand is to leave Jeannie feeling drained. She was already tired from her time in Rome, and Rosa's visit has aroused emotions that stirred her own sense of un-fulfilment. The hot shower she'd promised herself as she made her way across Naples on this cold November evening is now too much of an effort to take. She washes her hands and face in a sink full of warm water, then she brushes her teeth. She's almost asleep before she gets into bed, but, in bed, it only seems a moment before she wakes with a start, with the thought that she's thinking about Rufus Mettius as a living person – alive somewhere at the moment.

For a little while she's wide awake. She wonders if Rosa made it to Perugia, and if she and Alfredo are now together. And, whilst moving her legs to warm the bed, she wonders when it will be her turn.

On her final visit to Rome, on the train there, she wonders if she really needs to stay over. If she were to forego one last visit to Ponte Fabricio – in the hope of catching a glimpse of Rufus Mettius there at dusk – she could come back on the early evening train. But, having already booked a room in a cheap hotel she's recently heard of, she decides to leave the matter open.

On arrival she does not hurry from the station as she had on all previous occasions. Instead, she decides to have a coffee and consult her street map. When she's done this, and visualised her planned route she wonders if she's slowing things down to make sure she has to stay over for the night.

Having had this thought, she decides she'd better get started.

At the first museum she visits – the smaller of the two on today's itinerary – she could easily be taken for a tourist who only has a passing interest in the exhibits. Her enquiries have told her that the few funerary plaques the museum possesses are all on display. She looks them over, searching for the words Rufus Mettius Diomedes at the same time as stealing herself against disappointment. And she's quite right to do so. None bears his name, and she has a second, more detailed look at the inscription to see if the plaque could possibly be his but under a different name. None corresponds to what she knows of Rufus Mettius's life and she leaves the smaller of today's museums after having been there for fewer than ten minutes.

It's almost twelve-thirty when she arrives at what she knows is her last chance of finding any trace of Rufus Mettius, and she's close on an hour-and-a-half early for the appointment she's made with the curator. She considers having lunch before she goes into the museum. But though her stomach feels empty, she decides that the thought of having lunch is just a way of putting off a moment of finality.

She shows her museum pass at the ticket office, then makes her way to the corridor where she's been told all the museum's funerary plaques are on display. Now excited by the sight of so many funerary plaques – and it seems she's saved the best till last – she walks past the first cluster in her eagerness to see the full extent of the collection. It's a few seconds before she realises that she's just passed a plaque bearing the name 'Rufus'. She hesitates, again steeling herself against disappointment, before taking the few steps back. When she dares look at the inscription and sees the name Rufus Mettius Diomedes, she tells herself it could be another person of the same name and she must not think she's actually found him. That is, unless every word of the inscription ties up with what she knows about him.

Then she reads the inscription, and again a second time to ensure the voice she's now hearing is the same one she hears when reading his scrolls.

And yes, every word carries the same intonation:

I, Rufus Mettius Diomedes, freeman of Naples, citizen of Rome, was happy that his journey was as long as he could make it. Eternally gratefully to Flavia who bore our three children, regretting only that I outlived her.

She writes this down, then records the years of Rufus Mettius's birth and death. She works out that he lived to be thirty-eight and her first thought is to hope this gave him time enough to see his children to early adulthood. Then she's completely thrown by the realisation that at the time the scrolls were written Rufus Mettius would have been fifteen at the most, and Flavia a girl of no more than twelve. The voice Jeannie has been hearing is that of a man in his late twenties, and the thought that he was just a boy is a shock that will take some getting used to.

She walks further along the corridor, glancing at the other funerary inscriptions, reading some in full – using them as a guide to the sentiments of Rome at this time. She returns several times to Rufus Mettius's plaque, each time wanting to trace its engraved letters with the tip of her extended forefinger, each time put off by the nearby custodian who's constantly watching, and she tells herself that it's not the feel of the still fresh stonemason's marks that's important, rather it's the way that Rufus Mettius's words have touched her.

Returning to the ticket office she writes a note for the curator, with whom she has an appointment an hour later. She asks the woman behind the glass screen to pass the message on. Then Jeannie leaves the museum, unsure, at first, of where she's going. Outside she decides to make one last visit to the ancient bridge Ponte Fabricio, but doesn't want to be there until it's nearly dusk, so she makes her way to the small hotel where she's booked a room. She leaves her overnight bag in her room, then goes to the restaurant a few doors down the street to have a late lunch.

She doesn't hurry the meal, thinking she'll hold out there till late afternoon. But it's not possible to be in one of the world's most beautiful cities on a bright early winter's day and not want to explore it, so, she makes her way to the Spanish Steps, walking unhurriedly along Via del Babuino before coming into Piazza de Spagna. She stands for a while in front of the Keats-Shelley Memorial House, thinking this a place she'll come back to when she's just a visitor to the city. Then, as she descends the Spanish Steps, there's the first sign that the light is fading, so she hurries towards Rome's central avenue, Via Del Corso. It's a long, wide street and try as she might she seems to be making little progress along it as the sky darkens. When she comes into Via Del Teatro

Di Marcello, she's hot and feeling hurried, but with the bridge in sight, and the sky still showing light, she's able to slow down knowing that she's made it.

Isola Tibernia, an island in the river, has two bridges linking it to the city either side of the Tiber, but for Jeannie it has just this one crossing. And coming over Ponte Fabricio, as dusk arrives, Jeannie realises that this is the last chance she'll have to see what her imagined Roman looks like. The rational side of her knows that this idea of seeing him is foolish, but there's the sense of a person within her, and she knows he's there if she could but see him. He's in his late twenties, he's been in Rome for several years now, and as she imagines him coming over the bridge, drawing his cloak about him on this chilly evening, she feels sure she'll know his face when he gets closer.

She's thinking that this face will resolve into one she recognises when a car pulls over. The window is lowered, and the driver calls in Italian, 'How much?'

With her head thrust towards the car she calls back, 'You are mistaken.' Then she hurries off.

Back in her room in the cheap hotel, Jeannie is acutely aware of how being mistaken for a street walker has brought her to her senses. She now wants to put loitering by the Tiber behind her and return to what needs be done. She knows she has an extraordinary fragment of history in her possession, and given that Rufus Mettius survived the eruption and had a life of his own, there's a fascinating story to be told. It's this that she now turns to, beginning with her handwritten copy of his funerary inscription.

But the inscription itself – and the fact that she's written it out by hand – is a lure to what she now regards as self-indulgence. So she quickly types the funerary inscription into her laptop, then neatly folds the notepaper on which she wrote it and puts this in her travel bag for safe keeping. In doing this she decides she must also resist writing out any more of her translations of Rufus Mettius' scrolls in longhand. When she turns back to her laptop it's to analyse the part of his inscription, where he says he was 'happy that his journey was as long as he could make it.'

The Director of Excavations assumed, as she did, that Rufus Mettius's ambition was to go to Rome to become a senator and thereby play a part in re-establishing the Republic. This was based on what Rufus Mettius had said in one of his scrolls. But on reflection, bearing in mind her more recent reading of the history of the period, it is impossible to believe that he could have realised such an ambition. The Senate was a closed order: membership was obtained either as a birth right or by imperial grant. Therefore, if Rufus Mettius had headed for the Senate it would have been to offer his services to a Senator, perhaps as a personal assistant or the administrator of a Senate committee. And, if so, if he had obtained such a position, he would have taken his career as far as he was able – and almost certainly secured a future for his children.

Whilst Jeannie has been considering this, she's also been vaguely aware of the sounds around her. Someone above has taken a shower, then another. In between there's been the same footfall on the stairs. And pricking up her ears, she's now aware of the rhythmic sound which seems to be coming through the ceiling. This is soon accompanied by a 'Ah, ah-ah, ah-ha-ha' from what sounds like an operatic singer. When this cycle is repeated ten minutes later it's difficult to avoid just one conclusion: this place is a bordello.

The only thing Jeannie has removed from her overnight bag is her laptop, and she now re-packs it. She has a look around the room to make sure it's exactly as she found it. Handing in her key at reception, she notices several men waiting in the small bar opposite the hotel.

'I've decided not to take the room after all,' she tells the woman on duty.

'Is all right, I understand,' is all the woman says, her expression unchanging.

Jeannie takes the late train back to Naples. It's been a long day, she's tired and the rhythm of the train is seductive. And it's fortunate that the late train terminates in Naples, where she's woken by a hand on her shoulder – a uniformed man pointing her in the direction of the station's exit.

In the vestibule of her apartment block, dead on her feet, she finds an envelope in her mailbox. It contains a postcard from Rosa. It reads, 'You were right!' followed by three large exclamation marks.

The next day Jeannie sees Angus as soon as he arrives on site. She tells him she's found Rufus Mettius' funerary inscription. She says it seems likely that he made it to the Senate as a citizen of Rome and a freeman of Naples.

'He married Flavia and they had three children,' she says.

'Amazing! Amazing!' exclaims Angus, adding: 'Why not go home for an early Christmas and write the guidebook?'

Chapter 6

Family matters

Finding Rufus Mettius's funerary inscription provides as good an ending for the guidebook as could have been hoped for. Not only that, this confirms that what happened in the course of Rufus Mettius's life is not only going to be at the core of the guidebook but will also be the basis of her research. And here, arising from the confident sense that her life now has both substance and direction, comes the idea that she'll be able to change her relationship with her family – and especially with her mother.

But this is for later.

She goes to the B&B hotel in Kelvingrove where, after several stays, the landlady Agnes and husband Gordon seem to have come to regard her as a surrogate daughter. They're pleased to tell her that her regular room is available, except for Christmas and New Year. This suits her just fine, she tells them, because she'll be spending the holiday with her family.

Then the question of contacting her mother arises. On the plane, she'd considered ringing her towards the end of the week

– as if from Italy – to say she'd be home in a couple of days. But the possibility of being seen in Glasgow, and this somehow getting back to her mother, argues against it. So she decides to ring home and invite herself over for Sunday lunch.

She gives careful thought as to what to say: 'Mum, guess what? The villa we're excavating is going to be made into a museum and I've got the job of writing the guidebook. So I've come back to work in the university library, here in Glasgow.'

'So you're back in Glasgow?'

'Yes, sorry I didn't let you know I was coming – it's all been rather sudden.' She hurriedly adds, 'How is everyone?' to change the subject.

'Everyone's fine, we would have let you know if they weren't. So when will we see you?'

'I thought I might come over on Sunday. How's that with you?'

'That's fine. Jamie and little Alastair were supposed to be coming over, but now they can't. So, you'll be here for lunch?'

'Yes, if that's all right.'

'And you'll be staying in Glasgow, I suppose, until Christmas?'

'Yes, I'll be with you for Christmas and New Year, if that's OK?'

'Aye, that's fine with me – I just need to be told.'

At a superficial level there's nothing much wrong with this conversation, but Jeannie hears all the intonations and inflexions and has the back-story to every little detail. To her mother saying, 'I just need to be told,' Jeannie could add, 'because I'm only the drudge round here.' And it's fine for Jeannie to come home for Sunday lunch now that her brother Jamie, youngest of the twins by exactly twelve minutes, and his boy Alastair aren't going to be there. Had they been, her presence would have been conditional: 'Would you try to get on with Jamie and have a nice word for little Alastair,' her mother might well have said to her. Also, there was no mention of Jamie's wife, Cassandra, who's unlikely to be there with Jamie and Alistair. She's an ambitious lawyer and needs to work on Sundays, especially if invited to her mother-in-law's for lunch. And when Cassandra doesn't turn up with Jamie and son for lunch – as is usually the case – Jeannie's mother makes excuses for her.

The other thing of note is her mother's response to being asked if everyone's all right. Her reply: 'Everyone's fine, we would have let you know if they weren't,' is a clear rebuke for Jeannie's lack of contact.

After this conversation Jeannie is immobilised for a little while, already having doubts about getting the relationship with her mother and family onto a new footing and realising that the presence of any one of her brothers – even if only in her mother's head – will likely be a spoiler. But she does not let these thoughts hold her up for long and soon returns to unpacking her bags in her room in the B&B hotel, putting her laptop and A4 notepad on the dresser top ready to take to the college library first thing on Monday morning.

Her intention is that she'll spend tomorrow, Saturday, doing her Christmas shopping, guided by the aim of getting on with her family. In the past, buying presents has been a problem. The fantasy of her teenage years was that she'd buy something like a tobacco pipe and a set of pipe cleaners for each of her three much older brothers, none of them a smoker. This to let them know how stuffy, old fashioned and disagreeable she found them. The compromise of the last few years has been that she's bought them a tartan tie apiece, a pair of tartan knitted gloves and a pair of tartan socks. This year she thinks a sets of toiletries for each is more likely to please them. Yes, a pack containing deodorant, splash-on body lotion, shower gel and shampoo should do nicely. Oh, and she'll do the same for her father. And she'll get a gift receipt for each in case they don't like the fragrances she's chosen and want to change them.

For her mother she'll buy a nice silk scarf.

With such a straightforward list, her shopping is easily done and after a meal in town she's back at her lodgings by early evening. As sometimes happens, a moment or two after she's come through the front door, landlady Agnes emerges from her ground floor flat at the back of the house. 'Oh, Jeannie, it is you,' she says, as if surprised to see her, 'Gordon and I thought you might like to come in for a Christmas drink That is, if you're not going out this evening.'

'Yes, thank you,' she says, trying to sound keen. 'I'll just put these in my room,' she adds, holding up the carrier bags.

She does not hurry. She's noticed how Agnes and Gordon are more cheerful as the day progresses. Their daughter's emigration to New Zealand soon after she'd got married has clearly made their days more difficult to get through without a drop or two of sherry.

She knocks lightly on the door. It's quickly opened, as if her landlady has been hovering behind it. Jeannie is not far into the room when Gordon hands her a large schooner of sherry, asking her to sit on the settee. She's joined there by Agnes, who holds up her glass for Gordon to fill. When Gordon is settled in his armchair he raises his own refilled glass, saying, 'Cheers.' Agnes does the same, and Jeannie clinks her glass with theirs.

Gordon turns up the sound on the television. 'It's a comedy we're watching. The couple are only flatmates, but they're really meant for each other, and the comedy is about how it never quite happens,' Agnes informs her.

'Aye,' says Gordon, 'and the couple's fathers are comic characters. His father's a working-class laddie, her dad's a posh snob and they're always at each other's throats – in a funny kind of way, o'course.'

In sipping from the large and wide brimmed sherry schooner Jeannie tries to ensure that finishing the drink will coincide with the end of the programme. It's not difficult to bring the two together, the show having an obvious structure. There's a tussle going on between the couple and there'll be another setback which will yet again affirm that they really are intended for each other. The female protagonist's father will do something to assert his superior status, but the man's father, in his rough and ready working-class way, will eventually triumph.

When the show is over, and the sherry drunk, Jeannie moves to the edge of her seat, intending to say that she's got her Christmas presents to wrap – to take home tomorrow. But there's no need to say this. Gordon leans forward to take the glass from her as Agnes says, 'Well it was nice that you could come in for your Christmas drink.'

She thanks them, feeling quite light-headed, saying how

much she enjoyed the programme. They seem content with their entertainment.

Sunday spent with her parents is not a success. It seems that her mother has persuaded her father to have a word, though this is clearly against his better judgment.

'Jeannie, do you not think you could let us know more about your comings and goings?'

'Did any of my brothers?'

'Well, no, I don't rightly think they did. But, Jeannie, you're a young woman.'

'Yes, I know that, Dad.'

'Have a word with your mother, would you?'

He shuffles off, saying he's just going to catch up with the news – and it's not yet eleven in the morning.

Prior to the discovery of her maternal ancestry, and the knowledge of where her looks came from, Jeannie had found several reasons to explain why she felt different. Her father's age, for a start, marked her out. At school open days he always seemed more like a visiting grandparent, pleased with her progress but not directly connected to it. Then there was the large age gap between her and her three brothers, Cameron, the eldest, being thirteen years older, and the twins, Andrew and Jamie, only one year behind him. And this, she thought, was why she felt like an extra in the family: an add-on, an outsider.

By the time she was twelve she'd reasoned that at this same age her brothers would have known the facts of life and it would have been a source of embarrassment to them to know that their parents did it – as evinced by the baby inside their mother's belly. She also found it easy to imagine that they'd have been squeamish at the sight of their mother breastfeeding, and they'd have been put out by the baby's crying. In any event, what seemed clear to Jeannie by her early teens was that her brothers did not cherish their little sister; they did not like and tease her, as she'd seen in other families.

And her mother, in ways unsubtle, treated the boys as if they were the more important.

Jeannie did not abandon these earlier explanations of being made to feel different when she found out about her ancestry; when she saw how much she was like the 'squaw' in the well-preserved old photo. Even if this new account of her difference fitted as snugly as the mittens, she still regarded her previous explanations as valid. But there was an important difference. This similarity of her looks to those of her maternal ancestor gave her identity a new and strong dimension: a well-formed sense of contact with her Native North American forebear.

In ignoring her father's request for her to have a word with her mother, Jeannie goes up to her room with this other mother as her companion.

She takes the cardboard box from under her bed. She takes out the coarse brown paper parcel containing the moccasins and mittens, the photograph of the 'squaw' and the once screwed-up note saying Archie wanted the boys sent back to Scotland. She removes these from the folds of paper together with Rufus Mettius's slim, carbonised tablet and the original copy of his scrolls she'd left there on her previous visit. To these she adds her handwritten copy of his funerary inscription. She repacks them all within the coarse paper, knowing this completes the set. And, in putting the cardboard box back beneath the bed, she's aware that this marks the setting aside of her feelings for her imagined Roman and her new intention of working on his scrolls with studious detachment.

She goes downstairs to the kitchen and offers to help with Sunday dinner. Her mother allows her to baste the roast and make the gravy, but only under close supervision. And though Jeannie offers to help serve the meal, her mother insists she sits at the table with her father. Afterwards, Jeannie offers to clear up, but her mother is keen for her to 'talk to Dad'.

'You don't very often get the chance,' Jeannie's mother tells her.

So, Jeannie goes to the front room where the television is on, with the sound turned down, and yet another news bulletin silently reporting the same things that her father is reading about in his Sunday paper.

'Would you like a piece of the paper?' he asks, adding, 'Here, have the main part, I can read it later.'

She takes it from him, saying 'Thanks.'

'Don't you read the papers much?'

'No, hardly at all,' Jeannie says, adding, 'I don't really find time.'

'Oh well you should, there's an important decision coming up.'

'What's that, independence?'

'Of course. We'll register you here so you can have a postal vote, if you're away at the time. Would you like that?'

'Yes, that would be fine.'

'Well, you don't sound too keen.'

At this moment Jeannie's mother comes in with the tea tray.

'And what are you two talking about?' she asks with feigned interest.

'The vote for independence,' says Jeannie as her father raises the newspaper to hide his face, knowing what's coming.

'Oh no, not that,' says his detractor. 'One side tries to frighten us by saying we'll be much worse off, the other promises milk and honey. I can tell you right now I won't be voting.'

'There should be a law against that,' is what emerges from behind the paper.

'And what good would that do? You'd just be dragooning people to the voting booth so they can spoil their ballot paper,' is Jeannie's mother's quick riposte, making Jeannie think she's underestimated her mother's good sense. But her father's reply, when it comes, invites reasoned consideration. 'Well, it's to be hoped that by the time they get to the voting booth they'll have made their minds up.'

Monday, first thing, and by the time Jeannie has reached her preferred place in the college library she's worked out that over the Christmas and New Year period she'll have six clear days in which to do her work on the guidebook. She thinks this should be more than enough, and it's possible that she'll be able to take some time out, but by 10.30, with nothing done, she begins to wonder.

She decides to take a coffee break and buy an easy-flow pen. After a consultation with the museum service's publicity department Angus said the villa's guidebook should have a short historical introduction, whose focus was Pax Romana, to put life at the villa into context. Next, Jeannie should introduce Rufus Mettius and his master Asinius as protagonists. Of Asinius, she should be brief in describing his lifestyle: his dinner parties and his story telling, his amending the record Rufus Mettius kept of his stories and his quips to make himself sound the best and Asinius keeping these scroll records of his triumphs alongside those of the greats of Ancient Greece. Of Rufus Mettius's life at the villa, she should go into detail; his life and that of those around him illustrating life in the Roman Empire at this time. She should speculate on how it might have been that he and Flavia came together after she was taken from the villa. Certainly, the guidebook should end on knowing what happened to him, quoting his funerary inscription. As to what extent the transcript of all five of Rufus Mettius' scrolls should be included, or added as an appendix, that would be left to Jeannie to recommend in preparing her draft.

In reflecting on this guidance over coffee, and wondering if the easy-flow pen really had been worth buying, Jeannie is able to spot her first problem: her desire to include the whole of the scroll in which Rufus Mettius describes his relationship with Flavia. And, she thinks, if she were to include that scroll why not also include the whole of the scroll where he describes his relationship with little Vibia?

The posing of this question is useful in that it provides her with a way forward. Were she to include one whole piece of Rufus Mettius's writing, one whole scroll, then why not include them all? Except that this would make the guidebook scroll top-heavy. As a result of this thought she thinks she should prepare a very short summary of each scroll, then, with the summaries spread out before her, she'll be able to decide how to proceed with them.

She returns to the library to do this:

Scroll One: Rufus Mettius's Personal Political Statement.

* *He introduces himself as a slave-scribe, regarding his master, Asinius, as 'in every way a useless creature'.*

* *He attributes Asinius's uselessness to his being an Epicurean whose aim is to achieve the maximum sensory pleasure within his circle, without consideration for others.*

* *RM describes himself as a Stoic, whose fundamental belief is that we are all part of a world ruled by universal law. Each individual is a 'microcosm' of the larger world, so natural law governs all mankind. In this way all are equal, even slaves, though the dominant do all in their power to deny this.*

* *He explains that there is a group of Stoics in the Senate who, in danger to themselves, advocate the return of the Republic and to their having their share of power in it. He cautions that in achieving such power, they might use it to their own advantage and in doing this become the new rulers – rather than democrats.*

Having completed this summary, and having read it through a couple of times, Jeannie is struck by how it's lost the impact of Rufus Mettius's own words. What's powerfully clear in reading the scroll is that what he's talking about in modern terms is the idea of equality of opportunity for all people, and it occurs to Jeannie that she'll need to say something about this as a footnote explaining how the Stoic position can be seen in contemporary politics.

With this in mind she packs up her laptop and makes her way to the other end of the library where the newspaper stand is located. She's familiar with the layout of the broadsheet papers from her father's habit of reading aloud from the ones he takes, and she goes straight to the editorial pages. Having read the editorials she then reads the leading articles. In doing this she hopes to see how the arguments about equal opportunities are handled on either side of the debate about Scottish independence – this to inform the comment she might make as a footnote to this scroll. More than two hours later, with the light outside the library now fading, she has discovered that neither side in the debate about independence appears to have concerns with what she thought would be a fundamental issue.

The next day she works on the summary of Rufus Mettius's third scroll. She's decided to skip the second scroll, where Rufus describes his relationship with Flavia, since she remains convinced she should quote this scroll in full. As to the third scroll, she's decided that her summary should be fuller than that of the first with the inclusion of quotes. This to preserve something of the power of Rufus Mettius's own words:

Scroll 3: Little Vibia and Child.

Soon after Flavia had been taken from the villa by Septimius, Vibia, now pregnant, also left to marry the roofer's son.

'I was wrong to suppose that little Vibia would be the kitchen maid for the family she married into, though I am sure the roofer's

wife worked her hard. But she had time enough to visit the villa and though I saw her only once during the period of her confinement the women of the household told me all about her.'

There follows a section on the different ways in which news of little Vibia is gossiped by the female slaves at the villa. One of the youngest, who was hostile to Flavia and possibly jealous of her, tells him: 'You aren't half missing out there, that Vibia's such a chirpy little thing.' An older woman at the villa, who RM says is the same age as the roofer's wife, tells him, 'You're well out of it Rufus, they've met their match with her I reckon.'

'After Flavia had gone, and before I was reconciled to this, I began to think about the time I had spent with little Vibia. It would, I think, be true to say that our congress was at her behest. From the moment I arrived at the villa, she initiated it by whispering in my ear in the atrium, and the frequency of her visits to my room always accorded to her wishes. It was whilst thinking about this, and that she had become pregnant so quickly by roofer's son, that I began thinking.

What if the child were mine?

And, How could I possibly know this?'

In the next section RM thinks aloud about how he might know if the child is his. His first thought is to confide in the oldest of the women at the villa in the hope that she will say, 'Leave it to me and I'll find out.' But he quickly realises that speaking to her will itself be the source of gossip, and any answer she gets from Vibia is likely to be unreliable. He considers trying to see Vibia himself and simply say, 'Is the child mine?' Again, he thinks his asking this will be the source of more tittle-tattle, and Vibia – 'out of the good sense she possesses' – will deny the child is his. So his only recourse is, in due course, to see if the child looks like him, and unlike the roofer's son.

'But the child would need be two or three, or even older, before I might be sure it looked like me. And by this time it would be too late to claim the child as mine. The most I would be able to do, if it was a girl brought to the villa, would be to show her acts of kindness. And if a boy, perhaps I might be asked to teach him to read and write. But a boy, at the age of six or seven, would already be like his so-called "father" in manner: coarse and raucous – and spitting in the street.'

Later in the day, first in the college library and afterwards in her room at the B&B hotel, Jeannie completes her work on Rufus Mettius' fourth scroll.

Scroll 4: Rufus Mettius plans his escape.

The reason for Rufus Mettius planning his escape is entirely to do with his thoughts about being father to Vibia's child.

'Were the child to obviously look like me by the time he or she was aged of two or three, or word put about that the child was mine, then Vibia and the child would be cast out. And what would I do then?'

He explains the situation at the villa. 'The only slave at the villa to get pregnant in my time here was sold in the market. The villa is not a home to any children, so there is no chance of Vibia returning with hers. In any case Vibia is now a freewoman, and if she and the child are thrown out, she will be "free" to make her own living. But the chances of her doing this other than by prostitution, or by begging, are close to zero.'

It is in thinking about this possibility that he first plans his escape: 'If Vibia and my child are thrown out I must leave this place without delay and take them with me. If, on the other hand, I alone am convinced that the child is mine but to be brought up by the roofer's son, I will leave the villa to avoid the anguish of being witness to this.'

It seems, from what he says, that he does, in fact, make a detailed plan of escape, but for his own protection he does not put this in writing, saying only: 'I have no shackles or scars to mark me out as a slave, and with a scribe's skills could get by in Naples until made a freeman of the city. Then go on to a greater place.'

This is where the scroll ends, leaving more than half the papyrus on which it's written blank. It seems likely that Rufus Mettius would have recorded what happened to Vibia and the child over the coming next few years had not the eruption of Vesuvius so profoundly changed all their lives, and brought death to so many.

The next day, back in the college library, Jeannie gets on with her summary of the fifth scroll. This one is unlike the previous four in that it's an overview of life at the villa, as if a record written for posterity, and Jeannie decides that it can be summarised as briefly as she did for the first, since it's quite factual.

Scroll 5: Life at the Villa.

How the household is run by the slaves – all female except Rufus Mettius – and visiting freemen:

*   Running the villa is divided into two categories: things done by freemen (tending the garden and maintaining the building) and things done by the domestic slaves, like cooking, cleaning and washing – except certain items of outdoor clothing sent to the fuller.*

* *RM explains how the household works to serve the demands of Asinius and he describes how the slaves satisfy their own needs. This is broken down into three categories:*

i *Food and lodging: all live under the same roof, but are 'roomed' according to their position in the household. Likewise, the basic food is prepared for all. Special items of food for banquets are for Asinius and his guests only, with the slaves eating what's left over and sampling the food in preparation.*

ii *Clothing: Rufus Mettius makes the generalisation that where a master takes pride in his own appearance, this may carry over into the dress of the household. All the women are adequately clothed and those 'serving' at banquets are dressed for the occasion.*

iii *Sex and pleasure: a clear distinction is made between how Asinius satisfies his desires and the way the rest of the household satisfy theirs. Asinius is supplied with young slave girls by an up-market service. But his greatest pleasure is boasting at his banquets: having RM record his quips, his aphorisms and stories – editing them later to sound better – and adding these to his large collection of scrolls by the Greek literary greats. The slave women of the household are open about the sex they choose to have, and where they get it. RM quotes the laundry maid telling her assistant, 'Try that young roofer, give him a cup of wine and take him to the outhouse. Lift your clothes and show him what you've got, you won't regret it.'*

Having summarised this, the final scroll, Jeannie has the

impulse to add a comment of her own:

In a slave society, and this applies to both Asinius and his slaves – though for very different reasons – there is a disconnect between sex, affection and possession.

For sex, Asinius has his supply of young girls who he chooses for their looks and performance. As for affection, the nearest thing to this for Asinius is the regard he seeks from those within his circle, and the fondness he has for the possession of his own self-image.

In the case of the slaves, this disconnect has an entirely different origin. They do not have control over their own lives and can have little or no expectation of an exclusive relationship which combines sex, affection and possession.

Jeannie does not immediately recognise the significance of what she's just written, but it's only a little while later, having read through the scroll summaries, that she realises that this idea of the disconnect between sex, affection and possession will be the basis of her research. And it's to celebrate this, and the fact that her work on the guidebook is going well and near to completion, that she decides to give herself a treat and go over to Edinburgh for the afternoon to visit the Scottish Colourist.

On the way over to Edinburgh's modern art gallery it occurs to her to wonder where the impulse to make this visit came from. It seems obvious that it must have something to do with Alex, the deceiver, with whom she'd made this visit several times over. And it feels strange when he comes to mind that there's no longer any anger or recrimination about the way he'd used and dumped her. No, not at all, for she now sees him with a sense of detachment.

It's as if she's looking into a rock pool, and he's there amongst the various creatures, awaiting the next tide and the escape into another pool, only to repeat what's in his nature.

In the gallery where most of the Colourists are hung Jeannie finds their paintings are as magical as ever, but she feels unsettled. The renewed sense that her life now has substance, now that she's alighted on her research topic, together with the detachment she's found in thinking about Alex, has made her impatient to get back to changing her relationship with her family, and especially with her mother. But to make the trip to Edinburgh worthwhile, and to enjoy the Scottish Colourists as much as they deserve, she makes a deal with herself that she declares under her breath: 'Enjoy the Colourists whilst you're here and tomorrow decide what to do with the second scroll concerning Rufus Mettius and Flavia, then go home the day after that.'

Her mother is pleased to see her. Unlike the last time she was home, her mother is grateful for help in the kitchen and within five minutes of being back Jeannie is given the job of getting the vegetables ready for Christmas dinner. This involves cleaning, cutting up and blanching the ones to be frozen. Jeannie doesn't object to this early preparation as she might once have, asking why they couldn't get the vegetables ready first thing on Christmas morning; no, now she gets on with her work, knowing that having the vegetables in the freezer will help her mother feel she's on top of her many other jobs. But Jeannie is not completely taken in by the kitchen camaraderie she's enjoying with her mother. She's all too familiar with the thought that as soon as any one of her brothers turns up, even if only in her mother's head, things will be entirely different.

So, in this prepared state of mind Jeannie is not surprised when her mother says: 'I hope you don't mind if we put you in the attic room for the holidays. It's had a make-over and we've put one of those oil-filled electric radiators in there for you.'

'No, I don't mind,' Jeannie replies, 'I'll move the stuff from my room when I've done the vegetables.'

'No need, dear,' her mother tells her, 'We've done that already.'

Whilst Jeannie knows she should not be surprised that they've made this move without consulting her, she is quite shocked. But it's not the news that she's been moved from her room that is of greatest concern but rather it's what they've done with the cardboard box beneath her bed. So at the first opportunity, using the need to take her overnight bag upstairs to her new room as the excuse, she leaves the kitchen to go to her bedroom.

There is no cause for alarm. The box is under the bed exactly as she left it, and nothing has been disturbed. It seems that her parents may no longer be aware of the parcel her mother discovered in her grandfather's attic, but for peace of mind Jeannie brings the box up to her new room in the attic here.

Whilst she's looking for the best place to keep it, it occurs to her to wonder why she's been moved. It's been usual for her twin brothers and their families to stay over on Christmas Eve, but previously this has not meant disturbing her. So why now? She has the impulse to go downstairs and ask, but then thinks better of it. Yes, she'll ask why she's been moved, but she'll do it casually with a 'By the way...' when the opportunity arises.

She puts the cardboard box in the lockable cupboard in the attic room. Then she unpacks her things. By the time this is done she's no longer in a hurry to go downstairs and for a while she looks out of the small attic window. From here she can see the oldest part of town with its dark grey slate roofs, then the housing estates with tiles of various shades of red and brown, then a cluster of what look like bungalows with roofs of a vague kind of green, and beyond that the countryside. This view reminds her that it's a small, self-contained place and she recalls her eagerness to leave. But looking over the rooftops, with a sense of no longer being a part of the town, she regrets so easily losing contact with the classmates who had once been her friends. So, when she goes downstairs, it's with the intention of doing something about this.

Her mother is in the kitchen. Jeannie begins her enquiries about her old school friends whilst she makes a cup of tea for her. Her mother is up to date on many of these old classmates. She knows what degrees several of these old friends got, and whether they've gone on to do higher degrees, or into work, or are taking a gap year and so on. But it's soon apparent that much, if not most of this has been gleaned from the local paper. Jeannie expresses surprise that her mother hasn't heard about the children she was at school with through her voluntary work in the charity shop.

'Jeannie, I don't work at the counter, I work in the back room, sorting and pricing, and we don't have time for all the comings and goings,' her mother tells her.

This feels like a rebuke, and perhaps it is, but Jeannie does not react, saying instead, and as casually as she can, 'Oh, by the way, the attic room's been done out very nicely, but I did just wonder why I'd been put there.'

'The boys asked if they could spend Christmas Eve night sleepover together,' her mother cheerily tells her, and it appears she thinks Jeannie will be as pleased about this as she is.

From this Jeannie understands that her two young nephews have the same command of her mother's affection as do their twin fathers. And this, together with the unwavering affection her mother shows for the eldest of her grandsons – teenager Andrew, son of Cameron – indicates to Jeannie what she's up against in changing her relationship with her family. She concludes that achieving this, especially with her mother, is going to be an uphill struggle, and one she should take a break from for the moment.

She excuses herself, saying she's got to make some phone calls, and goes to the attic room to pick up her laptop. Then she goes down to the desk in her bedroom to make the calls on her mobile. At the desk, she tries to rationalise the situation. Yes, she can perfectly well see why her two young nephews have been given her room for a shared sleepover since her room has a double bed, whereas the bed in the attic is only a generous single. And she shouldn't really mind giving up her room since she no longer lives here, and no longer regards it as her home. And it's not that she dislikes her young nephews; it's just that she resents the attention they're so constantly given.

Using social media, on her laptop, she's quickly able to track down two of the girls she was at school with. Neither had ever been her close friends, or friends of each other, and she makes separate arrangements to see them in town for coffee. Whilst talking to them on the phone she enquires about their other classmates and finds out that not many of them will be coming home for Christmas. The ones who are coming back will more likely be here for New Year, and there's talk of going over to Edinburgh for a reunion at the New Year's Eve street party.

Interestingly, when Jeannie has her separate meetings with each of these old classmates they tell the same story of two boys they were at primary and secondary school with. Each tells the story in more or less the same words:

'You remember Craig Harris, don't you, well he got married as soon as he graduated. And you remember his best friend Tony McKay – you remember when we were at primary school, they always had their arms round each other. Well, Tony was Craig's best man, as you might expect. They'd kept up contact all the way through uni, even though one was in Aberdeen and the other one in Norwich. I don't know which way round it was. Well, anyway, Tony waved Craig and his wife off for their honeymoon in July and he's not heard from him since. Not a word! And he doesn't even know where they live.'

On each occasion of the story's telling Jeannie says, 'Maybe Craig's wife didn't take a shine to Tony – maybe she's jealous of their friendship.' And the reply on each occasion: 'Yes, that's what I thought.'

The plan is for Jeannie's three brothers and their families to arrive at their parents' house during the latter part of Christmas Eve afternoon. There's a cold buffet under cling-film waiting, and

Jeannie will help keep it topped up so they can nibble and eat as they please; this will go on well into the evening. Jeannie's twin brothers, their wives and two children will arrive together in the minibus they've hired, and they'll be staying over. Cameron, her eldest brother, and family live the other side of town and will go back home for the night, but they'll return on Christmas day for dinner. The last bit of preparation Jeannie's mother makes is to remind Jeannie that she'd said she'll make an effort with her brothers – and with the boys.

The Christmas get-together is the big occasion of the year for Jeannie's parents. Each year it follows the same pattern. Her mother keeps an eye out for the twins' arrival, and when the minibus draws up she'll be quick to get to the front door and Jeannie's father will only be a shuffle or two behind her. These days Jeannie positions herself a little way along the hallway to greet her brothers, their wives and sons, after, that is, they've received a fusillade of fuss and kisses from her mother.

Since her two young nephews were about five Jeannie has taken to shaking their hands as they come along the hallway. She does this with a smile, and it's done out of a conscious effort to say: 'See, I exist.' There's no reason why the young boys should be interested in an aunt they hardly ever see, of course, and Jeannie knows this. It's just that the boys disregard her in the same way as do her brothers. The sameness of this behaviour is so striking that it invites the thought that it might be inherited. But Jeannie knows a thing or two about genetics, this subject being of increasing importance in forensic archaeology – in identifying the mix of *Homo sapiens* and Neanderthal DNA in North Europeans, for instance – and she knows that such behaviour is not inherited. No, it's an attitude that's been picked up from those around them.

Her mother is now peeping through the hall window, and, as the minibus swings into the drive she says: 'Open the door,' to Jeannie's father. Her twin brothers and their families enter as a gaggle, and it's from this melee of a welcome that the two young nephews break loose. They're about to run past Jeannie when she stops them.

'Boys,' she says, 'haven't you forgotten something?'

She holds out her hand, and as the first boy takes it she wishes him a happy Christmas. She has to remind him to wish her a happy Christmas in return, but her second young nephew needs no prompting. Released, they bound off, one saying, 'Let's go up to her room.'

Cameron and family arrive a little later. It's the same palaver at the front door and Jeannie notices that her eldest nephew, Andrew, is looking a bit pop-eyed over his mother's shoulder at the bulges he's seeing under his aunt's sweater. He's a big lad who's got a more than downy face, and here Jeannie spots her chance. He's the last to go past her, having observed how his aunt has greeted his mother and father. He's hesitant in taking her hand, and when Jeannie leans to kiss him on the cheek he says, 'Oh, aye' as if he wasn't sure this greeting would extend to him – but he's pleased that it does. Jeannie holds onto his hand a little longer than she'd prefer to – the palm being a wee bit clammy – as she tells him the boys have gone upstairs, to her room, and would he keep an eye on them from time to time, to make sure they don't wreck it.

'Aye, of course, Aunt Jeannie,' he says.

'There's no need to call me Aunt Jeannie now. Jeannie's fine.'

The lad immediately blushes: 'Oh, I don't think ma dad would like that.'

'Then call me Aunt Jeannie when he's around.'

'Aye,' he says, 'I'll just go and see what the boys are up to.'

Early on, everyone takes a plate full of food, except the two young cousins, who are too excited to eat, unless they can take what they want to Jeannie's room.

'Is that all right with you?' Jeannie's mother asks.

'Yes, of course,' Jeannie says.

During the rest of the evening the members of the extended family move between the living room and kitchen as they graze from the table. Jeannie notices that there's a definite tendency for her three sisters-in-law to stick together. She recalls how the last of the three to join the group – before she became one of its established members – had remarked to Jeannie that whenever three women get together and any one of them leaves the room, the other two will talk about her. It now appears that Jeannie is observing this fear in action, and she'll not have the chance to talk to any of her sisters-in-law on their own. So, she pulls up a chair to join them, and though they welcome her by asking how she is, and what she's been up to, their eyes glaze over when she tells them about her work at the excavation. But when Cassandra, wife of Jamie – the older of the twins by just twelve minutes – asks if Jeannie likes Italian men, the hen party comes to life.

'They're a bit short for my liking,' says one.

'That's only in the south,' says the other.

'Yes, in the north they're often fair and Germanic,' says the third.

'Nice!' says Cassandra with a coquettish smile.

When Jeannie notices brother Jamie making his way to the kitchen with an empty plate, she makes her excuses to leave the party, saying, 'I'm just going to make sure there's enough food on the table.'

'Jamie's such a gannet,' says Cassandra, loud enough for him to hear her.

In the kitchen Jamie is looking for the mini-quiches and Jeannie takes a plastic box from the fridge, asking how many he'd like.

'Who's going to eat all that lot?' says Jamie as he peers into the box.

'Anything that's not eaten by the end of the evening will go straight into the freezer. Apparently, Dad even likes sandwiches after they've been frozen.'

'Oh, does he really,' says Jamie.

A silence follows, and it's one that Jeannie decides to leave empty.

For a moment it looks as if Jamie will turn from her, but then it seems he can't leave without saying something. So again she waits. There's a considerable backlog of things he might touch on, much having happened since he last saw her. Her degree, for instance; he could congratulate her on doing so well, and for going on to do research, or for getting the work in Italy, saying something like, 'From what Mum said your job sounds really interesting.'

Yes, he could say something like that, if only to be polite.

But when Jamie does eventually speak it's to ask a question of such vagueness as to make Jeannie wonder if he knows anything about her.

'How are things going?' he says, without a show of any real interest.

Jeannie's reply is also vague, but it's an attempt to find out exactly what he's been told. 'Well, pretty well really. I graduated this summer and I have a job at an excavation in Italy. The work I'm doing will be the subject of my research.'

Another pause, and Jeannie considers what Jamie might say in response. He could say he'd heard she was working at the villa of a wealthy Roman and invite her to say more about it. Or, he could say, 'Yes, didn't you do well with your degree.' Probably he won't say this, since his own degree was a lower second. But surely he'll want to know what her research is about, or what she's actually doing at the excavation. But no, it's one small detail that he homes in on.

'Yes, Mum said you'd brought back some scrolls to be electronically read. She said you'd got a wooden tablet on which a slave confessed to killing his master. She said she didn't like it in the house.'

This is a kind of rebuke, there is no doubt about it, Jamie manfully protecting his mother. And, yes, it's true, her mother was spooked by the aluminium case in the hall and the mention of what Jeannie described as Rufus Mettius's confessional tablet within it. Yes, and Jeannie is disappointed that this appears to be the only thing her mother has told Jamie – and perhaps the rest of the family. But she tries to show neither hurt nor puzzlement, and picking up the plastic box of mini quiches she returns them to the refrigerator. When she turns it's to see Jamie going through the doorway.

On Boxing Day evening, they go to her eldest brother Cameron and wife Margaret's house on the other side of town. This is now a family tradition. But it's not only the family who are there these days. In fact, these days Jeannie's family are in a minority. In recent times, coinciding with Cameron's career rise to consultant at the town's general hospital, the number of other people coming to this get-together has increased considerably, and it feels like Jeannie's family are being squeezed out. Jeannie is aware that her parents are unhappy about this, each year saying this might be the last. Jeannie, on the other hand, has an interest in Cameron and Margaret's friends. They treat her as they might the sister of any other friend. They're not bound by any kind of family loyalty but regard her as a person in her own right. So over the last two or three years she's got to know some of them quite well, and they spend their time together sharing what they've been up to in the year that's almost over. They're interested to hear about her work, and what it's like at the excavation, and she's interested in what they tell her, though their talk is largely about their children, who are darting from room to room, and sometimes coming up to a parent to say something like, 'Mum, have you seen Maxine?'

As they return home in the minibus, the ordinary pleasantness of these ordinary conversations sets Jeannie thinking. It occurs to her that the indifference her brothers show towards her is not just passive. It's not simply that they're not interested in her, but more likely it's an active process of rejection, possibly to do with a culture of hostility they carry with them from childhood. And this ill disposition towards her is sustained by what she thinks of as the objective reality: that is, it is they, not she, who have always been favoured by their parents. Jeannie is inclined to think that their unchanging and unyielding attitude to her is worthy of a closer look, in just the same way that Asinius's active and continuous need to assert his ascendancy over Rufus Mettius invites examination. This parallel suggests to Jeannie that perhaps her research should be a comparative study: of now and then.

On New Year's Eve she has a thought which confirms this as the direction she should take. Frustrated in the attempt to change the relationship with her family, she leaves the house early to make her way to Edinburgh where she'll later meet up with some of the people she was at school with, at the city's street party. By late morning she's in the modern art gallery with the Scottish Colourists, and whilst looking at a catalogue of JD Fergusson's paintings she finds a portrait of a woman who's the spitting image of a slave girl in a mural removed from Herculaneum, now in the museum in Naples. The similarity of these images across the ages confirms that her research should be a study of now and then. It also raises the intriguing question of what Flavia might look like if she appears in any of the as yet uncovered murals at the excavation.

The group of ex-classmates spending New Year's Eve at Edinburgh's street party consists of four girls and just one boy. It's a pleasant enough night out as they go through the streets listening to the live bands and having drinks in various pubs. Well before the night is out Jeannie has swapped mobile numbers with them all and promised to stay in touch with the one called Cathy, who's taken a particular interest in her, reminding her that they sometimes played in the park together. Strangely, Jeannie has no recollection of this.

On the train home the lone boy, Antony, sleeps curled up in the corner seat. He's breathing heavily and not likely to hear as Cathy whispers to Jeannie, 'Antony's had a thing about you since we were in primary school. Didn't you know that?'

'No. What, since then?'

'Yes, he wants to know if he can call you?'

'Yes, of course,' says Jeannie, in no doubt that he won't.

On New Years' Day she has her parents to herself. She's late out of bed, and is feeling thick-headed, but she's thinking that sooner or later she's going to have to broach the subject of her relationship with her brothers. Over a lunch of leftovers, her mother tells her how much the boys – her two youngest nephews – enjoyed having her room on Christmas Eve, and they're making her a card to say, 'Thank you, Aunt Jeannie.'

This extinguishes the candle of hope she'd had about discussing her relationship with her family.

To be away from her parents on the day before her flight back to Italy, she decides to go into Glasgow. Her excuse is that she'll need to stay over at her B&B hotel so as to make the early morning flight to Naples.

Inevitably, her time on the train into Glasgow is spent thinking about what's happened over the Christmas and New Year holiday. She's pleased to have done enough work on the scrolls to be able to have a draft guidebook to present to Angus. And she's now clear about what she wants her research to be about, though not who'll supervise it – certainly not Professor Dinsdale. As for changing her relationship with her family, that's been a dismal failure and she thinks that the comfort eating resulting from this is the reason she's puts on so much weight. Nevertheless, she's going to treat herself to a lunch in a new place in Glasgow that she's heard of.

In the restaurant, the bar, where the orders for food are taken, looks like it has come straight from Italy – as do the staff. The main difference between this café-restaurant and the one near the scavi is that this one is much larger, with an ice cream counter and settees facing each other along the long sidewall. When Jeannie places her order at the bar, she's asked to take her drink to wherever she'd like to sit and told the waiter will find her.

As she makes her way towards an empty table she feels exposed amongst a sea of faces. Immediately before she gets to the table where she's heading a man looks up, and his expression immediately changes. She would have walked past him unnoticed except that he says, 'It's Jeannie, isn't it?'

She turns to see who's just spoken, and though his face is familiar she can't immediately place him. Her first thought is that he must be one of the lecturers in the archaeology department, and someone she only knew at a distance, but he asks, 'How are you?' as if he knows her.

She's flustered by his being so familiar and not knowing who he is. She says, 'I'm fine... Yes, I'm fine,' giving herself a moment to think.

'Won't you join me?'

'Yes,' she says, thinking she'll have remembered who he is by the time she's sitting down.

He waits until she's put her drink down. And he waits again until she's seated before he says: 'It's Will, Young Will I think they called me.'

'Of course,' she says, as if to say, 'Of course I knew that,' and the thought that comes to mind, the thought that seems to completely fill her head, is to say: 'You've not changed. Not a bit,' and she has the desire to tell him this, and to add: 'And I've caught up.' It's the only thing she can think of, and it's not simply about uttering these words, it's something else as well, and she must find something else to say before he thinks she's dumb and witless. But this one thought will not be dislodged, until a little girl – who seems to have come from nowhere – puts her hands on his arm, saying:

'Daddy, I can't make my mind up about which ice cream to have.'

It's in seeing him giving his attention to the child that Jeannie has the chance to come to her senses.

'Which ones are your favourites?' he asks.

'Coconut and strawberry,' she tells him.

'Well, why not ask the man at the ice cream counter if you can have a tiny taste of each – to help you make your mind up?'

'All right,' she says, about to leave. Then she turns to Jeannie. 'Are you my daddy's girlfriend?' she asks without fear or hesitation.

'Oh, Bella, please!' her father says, before urging her back to the ice cream counter. She's reluctant to leave without an answer, and Jeannie is suddenly aware of why this little girl is so familiar: she's so much like Jeannie was herself in a photograph taken on her fifth birthday. She wants to tell him this, but it seems there's something he needs to say before she speaks.

'Sorry. Sorry about that,' he says. 'Since Bella's mother remarried, Bella's one aim in life is for me to do the same.'

Silence. For a moment – and for both – it's as if all sound in the restaurant has ceased.

'Sorry, I just thought I should explain that,' he tells her.

Jeannie casts a glance at Bella, who's now at the ice cream counter. Her one thought now is how lovely she is, and she turns to tell him this.

'Yes... Yes, she is,' he replies and then hesitates, and it seems he's now the one who's tongue-tied. As, in fact, he is. Something that must have been obvious to him for years now has just crystallised with astonishing clarity. An impossible infatuation with a schoolgirl made him move jobs much earlier than intended and in meeting Bella's mother he imagined he'd found the woman Jeannie would become.

She's looking at him, she's waiting, and he feels he must say something.

'Soon after we married, and Bella's mother was already pregnant, we realised we weren't suited.'

Bella returns to break the spell.

'Have you decided which ice cream to have?' he asks.

'Yes,' she says.

'Which one have you chosen?'

First giving Jeannie what seems a meaningful look, and then doing the same to her father, she says, 'I want strawberry and coconut, together.'

It's impossible to tell whether she means that she wants them to be together, or it's just the chance coincidence of words and glances that suggests this. And either Will does not recognise this possibility, or chooses to ignore it, for he quickly says: 'Is that right? Did the man say you could have half-and-half?'

'Yes, can I have the money now please?'

Taking a five-pound note from his wallet, and raising an eyebrow at Jeannie, he says, 'Can you bring the change back straight away, please?'

Bella takes the money from him and matter-of-factly speaks to them both, asking, 'Have you made your minds up yet?'

'Bella!' her father remonstrates, but gently. 'You can't ask things like that.'

'Why not? You've been talking for ages.'

'Bella, this is Jeannie, I was her...' He stops abruptly, then adds, 'We're just catching up.' Bella gives them both a long look, and he says, 'Go and get your ice cream, would you.'

So, catching up it is, and Will is quick to ask Jeannie if she did the degree in archaeology, as planned.

'Yes, specialising in forensics as you suggested,' she reminds him.

'Yes, of course,' he says, remembering talking to her about this.

'I'm working in Italy, between Pompeii and Herculaneum.'

'Really?' he says, wanting to know all about it. And in the next few minutes she tells him about her work. But what's important about this conversation, whilst Jeannie is doing the talking, is that his gaze keeps falling upon her lips and she remembers how it was like this in the classroom – but she now understands its meaning.

Soon enough Bella is back. She's clutching the change in one hand and the ice cream in the other. She's in quite a mess, with ice cream running down her arm and dress.

'Oh, Bella, what will your mother say when she sees you?' Will quickly takes the two paper napkins from the table, wrapping one round the cone, which he asks Jeannie to hold. With the other he cleans up Bella, first wiping round her mouth, then her hand and arm, saying, 'You know she'll be here at any moment.'

Bella looks a little shame faced, but she's smiling at Jeannie over her father's shoulder as he wipes her dress and she mouths in a whisper, 'Have you made your minds up?'

Jeannie's reply is also whispered: 'No, not yet. But we will.'

'What's that?' he says, still dabbing at Bella's dress.

But neither answers.

With the cornet returned, Bella shows her approval of Jeannie by licking the ice cream and smiling at her intently. She's only just finished eating the last of the cone when she's jumping up and down, calling, 'Mummy, Mummy.'

Jeannie notices Will's face suddenly change, and she looks across the room to see the cause. Bella's mother is a woman of striking appearance, the black trim of her camel coat picking up the darkness of her hair and eyes. Seeing Jeannie looking in her direction, she smiles. It's an impassive smile of neither greeting nor hostility, or even curiosity, that seems to say, 'Good luck, but don't tell me anything about it.'

'Should I move away for a moment?' Jeannie offers.

'No, please stay,' he says, adding, 'She won't come any closer.'

He hands Bella her small overnight bag from the other side of the table, then leans to kiss her.

'Can I kiss her as well?' Bella asks.

'Her name is Jeannie, and you'd better ask.'

So, Jeannie receives a wet kiss on her lips and Bella is gone, jumping and waving in the doorway one last time before she leaves.

Alone, and together, Will returns to where they'd left off, skirting what's now obvious to them both. 'You said the research you had in mind was outside the scope of archaeology.'

'Yes, I think it's really social anthropology.'

'Do you remember me telling you about the social history research I was doing?'

'Yes. About your great-great-grandfather,' she says.

'Well, soon after I'd told you about that I had the same thought and switched to the social anthropology department. My tutor was called Dr Pamela Newlyn, and I'm sure you'll like her.'

For each, this is the resumption of a conversation begun years earlier – but now not in the classroom. And it's Jeannie who has the concluding words, in saying, 'Yes, I'm sure I'll like Dr Pamela Newlyn, if you did.'

They leave the café-restaurant soon after Jeannie has told him she's booked on a flight to Naples first thing tomorrow morning. They go to the B&B hotel to pick up her things and then go on to stay at Will's place. Early the next day he takes her to the airport.

Chapter 7

Conclusions

She finds Angus behind his desk in the site office. He looks up and makes brief eye contact, but does not appear to see her.

'Happy New Year,' she says, to gain his attention.

'Och, aye,' he says, possibly with intended good humour.

'Did you have a good Christmas?'

'Yes... yes, we did,' he says slowly, and without looking up.

She waits until he's ready to talk, the draft copy of the guidebook in her hand. When he looks up, and when he speaks, there's no acknowledgement of the fact that she's been away from the excavation for more than three weeks.

'The civil engineers undertaking the project will be coming on site next week and I'll need to be freed up to deal with them. Our two elderly volunteers are working through the winter and will need supervising. Also, the mural conservation team are coming on site before the end of the month and you'll need to liaise with them before they get here. Then there's the admin to deal with for the students on site placement – they start two weeks before Easter – and opening up the hostel will need sorting...'

Before Angus has run through all the things on his list, it's become obvious that this is Jeannie's new job description he's dealing with, and she feels impelled to ask: 'What about Giorgio, shouldn't these be his jobs?'

'Giorgio's got a site of his own,' Angus says, without further comment.

'Oh, right... that's news then.'

'No, not really. He's been angling after his own site for ages,' he tells her, as if it's of no interest to him.

Having said this, Angus presses on with the list of jobs he wants her to do, and it becomes apparent that she's being put in charge of all the remaining archaeological work on site, as well as looking after the students. Now is not the time to tell him about her plans, nor about Will, so, when Angus is done, she says, 'That's fine,' and she means it.

Her plan, formulated on the plane, was to tell Angus about her intended research and say that she'll be moving away from archaeology whilst at the same time re-assuring him that she'll stay on here to see the project through – or at least until the end of next summer. But this sudden change of fortune is both interesting and exciting. And it's as a result of this that Jeannie begins to reconsider what had seemed so settled when she entered the site office.

With Will she's sure she's found the missing part of her life. He'll be bringing Bella to stay with her in Naples during the next half-term school holiday, and she's looking forward to this. She's sure they'll be a new family. But on what terms? This sudden turn-about at the scavi – and more particularly the news of the mural restoration team's imminent arrival – has revived her interest in archaeology. She'll not be able to have a proper relationship with Will and Bella at this distance, of course, but there's the possibility that she could go on to managing excavations in Scotland.

It's something she'll have to consider.

The mural restoration team of four people is despatched from Naples at the end of January, as promised. At her first site meeting with them it's decided that they'll work on two fronts. These are the scriptorium where they think it looks like the walls are decorated with scenes from Greek antiquity, and the room where Asinius did his entertaining – where it seems his lavish lifestyle is illustrated. Jeannie is invited to join the team when she can find the time, working under their supervision and standing in for any team member who needs to visit another site, as sometimes happens.

She works long days at the scavi, sometimes coming in at the weekends. And in the six weeks before Will's visit she finds time to search out places to take Bella, and makes plans for the five days they'll be together. Whilst travelling on the train between Naples and the villa she sometimes gives thought to her own future. She thinks managing an excavation may be something to which she's well suited, but she does wonder if this may only be true of Italy, where there are so many sites rich in artefacts yet to be uncovered. The prospect of this same kind of work in Scotland is less attractive. There the archaeological sites are more likely to consists of only the foundations of buildings, the odd coin and plentiful pieces of broken pottery. The abundance of burial sites there, and skeletons, together with the possibility of complete bodies in acidic bog-land is, she supposes, something to celebrate, but she's not really that attracted to it.

All such thoughts are put aside when she meets Will and Bella at the airport. Bella runs to her calling, 'Jeannie, Jeannie!' and when Jeannie kneels to give her a hug Bella throws her arms around her neck, saying, 'You're my daddy's girlfriend, aren't you?'

When she stands to embrace Will there is no doubt that it's him she's intended to be with.

On the third day of the visit, they go to the scavi, 'to see what Jeannie does there,' Will tells Bella. On the way, on the train, Bella has a window seat next to Jeannie and she's quietly content to look at the countryside that's passing by until she gets her first sight of Vesuvius.

'Is that it?' she asks, turning excitedly to Jeannie.

'Yes, that's Vesuvius.'

'Tell me what happened.'

For a second time Jeannie gives Bella an abridged version of the event, omitting to tell her about the people who were trapped, having already decided that it will be best to avoid the scriptorium and plaster cast of Asinius' body when they get to the excavation. She tells Bella that after several days, when the ground shook, what they thought was a mountain suddenly exploded and the red-hot larva from inside was sent high into the air, shattering into tiny pieces of ash and pumice as it smashed into the freezing cold air high up in the sky. This made a really big dark cloud and when the pieces of ash and pumice began to come down the people knew it was time to leave. The eruption went on for nearly five days and when all the ash and pumice settled it completely covered all the buildings.

For a second time Bella listens to this with amazed wide eyes. And for a second time Bella asks, 'Will it happen again?'

'It might, but not for a long time yet – and definitely not whilst we're here.'

They begin their tour of the villa at the still intact plank seat the Three Girls of Naples had put together. Jeannie explains that the great mound of crumbled ash and pumice will be bulldozed over the area where the portable cabins are now situated, and this is where the café and picnic area will be built – overlooking the villa museum. She's explaining how the scriptorium will be overarched by a sweeping glass structure as Angus approaches. Bella has not been listening to this, but rather trying out the springiness of the plank seat, and seeing Angus, she jumps off and runs towards him.

'You must be Bella,' he says.

'Are you Angus?' she asks.

'Yes,' he says, 'I expect the grown-ups are being boring.'

After being introduced to Will, Angus takes holds of Bella's hand, saying, 'Shall we go and have a look at what Jeannie's been doing?'

He leads the way, speaking in a loud voice as if talking to Bella, but all the while tossing the words over his shoulder: 'Ahead, to the side of the villa, will be the exhibition centre where the visitors get their tickets and the guidebook Jeannie's been writing. Then, when they've bought their tickets, they'll enter the villa here, through this fine front entrance. Reproduction doors are being made using the carbonised sections we recovered as a template.'

Angus then leads them to what, for Bella's benefit, he calls 'the dining room, where they had their big dinners.'

The two members of the mural restoration team working here have made good progress and they stand back to show their visitors what they've revealed. There's the upper body and head of a girl holding a bowl of grapes. She's looking down – possibly at a figure on a cushioned platform. 'We think she's a slave girl called Flavia,' Angus tells Will, adding, 'Well, that's what one of the scrolls which Jeannie's translated seems to suggest.'

'She's a real Roman beauty,' is Will's only comment.

'Yes,' Angus agrees, adding: 'Regrettably, for her, it's more than grapes that she'll be serving.'

Whilst they're looking at the other part of the mural so far restored, Jeannie does not say a word. When she'd first seen the image of what they think is Flavia she was shocked. For some reason she'd imagined her as fair haired, and perhaps of northern origin. But this Flavia is a classic Roman beauty. Her eyes are brown and large, her hair is interlaced with fine braid, and though she's only a child her poise is dignified. And having seen Flavia in what seems like the flesh Jeannie keeps hoping an image of Rufus Mettius won't be found, fearing what she might see in his eyes.

But now is not the time to dwell on this. Angus is moving towards the scriptorium, keen to show Will and Bella the reproduction furniture that's been put there.

'It's an exact copy of what was here, and exactly where it was,' Angus tells them.

Bella is allowed to sit on a Roman couch as Will tries out a seat resembling a piano stool. It's only as they're leaving the scriptorium that Angus says, 'Oh, yes, and there's Asinius. We think he was killed when the roof caved in, hit on the head by a large roof tile before he was covered in ash and pumice.'

They all stand around the plaster cast.

'Was that a man?' Bella asks.

'It was, that's the shape of him,' Angus confirms.

Bella asks nothing more, appearing to take the cast of a dead man in her stride as she moves on, now in the lead. Jeannie is briefly halted, looking down on Asinius. She knows exactly how he died, or believes she does, and it's not the way just described.

For Jeannie, the weeks in the run-up to Easter go more slowly than the previous six. The mural restoration team completes its work and Jeannie is relieved to find that Rufus Mettius is not witness to Flavia's forced service. Re-opening the hostel and overseeing the arrival of a dozen students from various parts of the world keeps her busy. But there's space in her life for other thoughts. And what preoccupies her most is the return to thinking about her research.

Having given it no thought for several weeks it would seem that the idea of the disconnect between sex, affection and possession has lost much of the potency it had when it first came to mind. Or maybe it's that this idea has become so familiar as to now seem ordinary. Yet again, perhaps it was not such a good idea in the first place.

It's hard to tell.

Another recurrent thought is about Angus. He'd taken to Bella, and she to him in the short time she was at the scavi and Jeannie had been struck by the thought of what a good father he'd make. With his being gay, she's been curious about the civil law in Italy and the possibility of a surrogate pregnancy, or adoption, and she's wondering if she could say something to him about this. But, of course, she can't, unless he raises the subject first and in the weeks in the run up to Easter, he doesn't, and she eventually loses track of this thought altogether.

By email, and by phone, it's arranged that on the Saturday they'll travel to Rome and stay over until Tuesday. The idea is that they'll witness the Pope addressing the massed pilgrims in their many languages, his voice transmitted over the huge square of St Peter by loudspeaker. It's not that either Will or Jeannie is religious, but this is a grand spectacle which visitors to Rome should not miss if they happen to be there on Easter Sunday.

After they've left their bags in their hotel room, and had an early lunch, Jeannie begins to show Will the Rome she knows. They go first to the Spanish Steps – where else? After they've gone up the steps, and are in Piazza de Spagna, she tells him she always intended to go into the Keats-Shelley Memorial House, but never wanted to do so on her own. So they go in. It provides an agreeable start to their visit, but nothing more than that.

Will has the idea that it would be good to go to some of the well-known places Jeannie has mentioned on three of Rome's seven hills – this to get the feel of the ancient city. They do this over the next few hours, returning to the Spanish Steps in the late afternoon. This time they descend the steps and Jeannie leads the way to Via Del Corso. Along this broad avenue they buy sandwiches to keep them going until the dinner they've planned in a little restaurant near their hotel. A short while later they go along Via Del Teatro Di Marcello, and the light is fading as they make their way to Isola Tibernia.

On Ponte Fabricio, exactly halfway over the bridge, Jeannie stops and steps back from Will.

'What is it?' he says.

'You are the one I wanted to see here,' she tells him.

'And what does that mean?' he asks, now smiling with her.

'That is my secret.'

It is a secret Jeannie will keep. It belongs with the moccasins and mittens, the once screwed up note, the photograph of the 'squaw', the copy of Rufus Mettius's scrolls and his carbonised tablet.

It is a place that during her life Jeannie will sometimes visit.

It is her heritage.

And before she sleeps on this first night together in Rome, which she knows to be as good as life can give her, she goes there. She sees the squaw's gentle gaze and the open hand that directs the eye towards the things she's made. She sees that this woman would have known days and nights such as this, and she knows she gave up her boys for their better future – that otherwise she would have been fierce to keep them.

And after this, Jeannie knows exactly what to do with her life.

Three days later, after accompanying Will and Bella to Naples Airport, she returns to her apartment in the city. She sends an email to Dr Pamela Newlyn in the university's social anthropology department. A week later, and at her own expense, she returns to

Scotland, having promised Angus she'll return to see the project through to its end.

By the time she meets Pamela Newlyn they've exchanged emails and had a telephone conversation, so their appointment is largely about shaking hands on their agreement. They meet in her room in college, lit by bright spring sunshine. Jeannie is immediately struck by Dr Newlyn's appearance. She's wearing the simplest of clothes: a cardigan that fits neatly into her waistline, with well-cut black pleated trousers and low-heeled black courts. She has a manner that is quiet, easy and reassuring, and she carries about her the sense that she knows exactly what she's doing. Jeannie can't help but think that this is the first person she's ever met who she'd want to be like. This thought keeps coming to mind as a distraction and it's as well that Dr Newlyn is only going over things already said and agreed – to make sure Jeannie is happy with them.

The other thing that keeps coming into Jeannie's mind is that maybe there was more to the relationship between Pamela and Will than her simply having been his tutor, something more than Will has chosen to mention. But she's able to brush this aside with the thought that Will would not have recommended her if there had been. And Jeannie is able to say, and to show in her demeanour, that everything is, indeed, agreed.

Yes, she understands the need to do the master's degree in Social Anthropology before she can register for a doctorate in the faculty. In that way she's more likely to get a lectureship at the university – if that's what she wants. The dissertation she'll need to do for her masters' degree will be based on the scrolls and will form the basis of her doctoral research; in that way she could get the whole thing done in just three years.

Dr Newlyn brings their conversation to a close by saying how much she's looking forward to supervising the research, adding how intriguing the scrolls are – how they speak to you as if they'd just been written. She adds one final thought before Jeannie departs: 'Yes, it will be fascinating to see if the disconnect of sex, affection and possession found in Rome's slave society have their parallel in contemporary culture.'

Jeannie goes straight back to Will's house, a place she will now call her own. She's impatient for him to return, forgetting that he'll be a little late because they've got Bella for the weekend, and he'll have gone to pick her up.

Whilst she's waiting, she wonders what she should tell him. That she now feels entirely resolved? That she feels like a person at the beginning of the rest of their life? That she feels completely happy?

When they get back it's Bella who comes in first, shouting, 'Jeannie, Jeannie!' Jeannie kneels to embrace her, and as she picks her up Bella clings to her tightly, saying, 'You're going to be my other mummy now, aren't you?'

Will says, 'Sorry, it's all she's talked about since I came back from Naples.'

Over Bella's shoulder, Jeannie asks how Bella's mother will take to her being called her 'other mummy'. Will says it's fine, Bella calls Calvino her 'other daddy'. So Jeannie carries Bella, still clinging to her, into the kitchen. She pulls a chair from under the table and sits with her. When Bella is settled on her lap Jeannie says, 'So, you're to call me Jeannie, and tell your friends that I'm your other mummy?'

'Yes,' she says, and no more than that.

'OK, let's have a high-five.'

Bella gives Jeannie a high-five and then slides from her knee, asking her father if she can watch CBeebies.

When Will returns from putting on Bella's favourite television programme, he asks Jeannie how she got on with Pamela Newlyn.

'Great. Fantastic. It's all agreed. I really like her,' is all she needs tell him.

After breakfast the next morning they drive to Jeannie's parents' house for Will and Bella to meet them and stay over for the weekend.

From the moment Will and Bella come into the family Jeannie's relationship with her parents changes, and it's immediately clear to Jeannie that this change will be the subject of her first assignment on the master's degree course. Yes, its focus will be on the way in which the introduction of the man – and future husband – into the traditional family changes both the daughter's standing and the family dynamic. And even before undertaking this assignment she can see that she'll be practising the skills of the engaged observer, as is asked for in the course notes.

But the change that will matter most to Jeannie – and it's a change that she will come to understand better through her studies – is in the relationship with her mother. For her mother takes to Bella as her first granddaughter, just as Jeannie has taken to her as her 'other mother'. And what makes this shared experience so forgiving is Jeannie's realisation that the attention her mother gives to Bella is the same as she would have given to her, had she been able.

On the first Sunday of this newly formed extended family – and having her own home to go back to – Jeannie takes what remains of her belongings from her parent's house. In fact, there's not much to take, apart from the cardboard box under the bed.

Except for one occasion when Angus sent her a postcard, Jeannie has given little thought to the villa-museum in the Bay of Naples, but during the late stage of her pregnancy her thoughts have returned there as she takes her afternoon rest.

During these rests she seems not to sleep, neither is she fully awake, and though her thoughts can seem highly lucid they are also inclined to wander. And it's in this state of almost sleep that she's been having thoughts about Rufus Mettius, thoughts that somehow seem to relate to the feelings of protection she has towards the life growing inside her. But the thought that underlies all this – and it's a thought that seems to demand an answer – concerns why she kept his carbonised tablet, and what to do about it.

On this particular afternoon, as she goes upstairs to take her rest, she is aware that there are two Jeannies at work here. There's the mother-to-be who intuits that the thoughts she's been having are bound up with the feelings of protection she has for the child inside her, and then there's Jeannie the social anthropologist, who inevitably must be a sceptic. But when Jeannie gets onto the bed, when she arranges the pillows to support her back, and when the baby kicks, it's just one voice who speaks: 'Won't you come out soon little one, so I can see who you look like?'

If it's a girl she hopes she will grow to look like Bella, which in its way is like saying she hopes the child will look like her – though she's not thinking this directly. She has a near-dread that the baby will look like one of her brothers, or her elderly father, but she reassures herself with the thought that whether it's a boy or a girl it's more likely to look like Will. Yes, and she recalls how soon after they were married she'd pored over his family photograph albums and found the same features tumbling through the generations in just the same way as she'd seen in Rosa's collection of pictures.

She lays back, alert now, waiting for the baby to kick again.

When it does, she thinks of Rosa and wonders if she has any children. She knows there's no way of knowing this, and even if she'd kept in touch with Angus he would have been unlikely to be able to tell her anything about Rosa.

For a little while, she wonders if she should have kept in contact with him. Then she remembers why she hasn't. She was put off by the picture postcard he sent of himself in front of the villa museum, where he's been the curator since its inception. There he is, in her mind's eye, in his full Highlander dress, and his message a one-liner: 'I'm going to get a lightweight kilt made for the summer!' Then she has a sudden insight. Yes, of course! The reason for his losing interest in the Greek writers of antiquity – in his finding fame in the discovery of a previously unknown piece of Greek writing – coincided with the decision to make the villa into a museum and Angus marking himself down as its curator. Yes! Forget the fame of finding a lost Rembrandt in the attic, Angus the showman-curator wears his full Highlander kit at the entrance to the villa and in this way gets the attention he craves – this time from the visitors!

She lies back, finding this thought tiring – or is it tiresome? And soon her thoughts return to Rufus Mettius.

It's to ask which story, which 'narrative' in the current argot, should prevail at the villa. The story that's told in the guidebook is of a slave-scribe who escaped Vesuvius's fury and found freedom and citizenship in Naples before going on to Rome and a position in the Senate. It's also about the master, Asinius, self-indulgent and vainglorious, who could not be parted from his own scrolls lodged alongside those of the Greek literary greats. It's about how he clutched these scrolls to his himself as the ash and pumice piled on the villa, bringing down the roof tile that killed him. And it's about how his body was lightly cooked by the first of the pyroclastic waves, then, with his clothes only singed, he was covered by a protective layer of ash and pumice before the final wave of flesh-devouring superheated gas descended from the volcano.

But this is not the truth as Jeannie knows it. Rufus Mettius thought he'd killed Asinius, and he'd done this to survive and have a life of his own. His writing says this. But why, with the other slaves all gone and terror all around him, did he hold back long enough to write a message on the wooden tablet? For Jeannie, now thinking with what feels like absolute clarity, it's definitely not a confession but a statement, and a statement that can only have one meaning: if the pursuit of one person's gratification prevents the lives of others being lived, then this should be thought of as life-taking and resisted by means equal to it.

With this thought now settled in her mind, the problem Jeannie now faces is how to ensure the message Rufus Mettius left on the wooden tablet is correctly interpreted. She could send the carbonised tablet to Angus. She could say she'd put it to one side whilst cleaning up Rufus Mettius's scrolls and forgotten all about it. She could say she was sorry about this, and, in the same covering letter, suggest how the message should be understood.

Yes, she could easily say this in two questions:

Why did Rufus Mettius take the time, and the trouble, to write his note on the wooden tablet when he could have just fled the scene?

Why did he carefully place the tablet next to his scrolls in the hidden niche when ash and pumice were raining down on the villa, and the other slaves all gone, if not to leave a message for posterity?

But even as she's thinking this, she's sure she knows what the museum's publicity department in Naples will make of Rufus Mettius's carbonised wooden tablet. Without doubt, they'll provide a lurid tabloid headline to boost visitor numbers at the villa:

Two Thousand Year Old Crime Solved!
A wooden tablet has been discovered on which a
slave confesses to killing his master ... etc, etc.

She lies back, disturbed by the thought that this could happen. And she's sighing as she looks at the bedside clock. It's almost 3 p.m. and for a moment this has no significance. Then she remembers that Will's interview is set for three, and she'd said she'd be thinking about him. So, this is what she does. She wonders, again, if it was wise of him to put just one short sentence in the large space available to explain why he wanted the headship. But on reflection, his saying, 'Headship is the best place from which to put my ideas about education into practice,' has secured him an interview for a job he really wants, and this short sentence makes it likely there'll be just one leading question.

Recalling the nervous kiss he gave her this morning, she smiles to herself, and in recalling the lightness of the touch of his lips on hers, the answer to her problem comes into mind as if it has just floated through an open window:

The tablet is where it belongs.

It is with the moccasins and mittens, with the photograph of her great-great-grandmother who she so much resembles, with the once screwed-up note telling of her great-great-grandfather's wishes, and with the original copy of Rufus Mettius's scrolls.

She is reassured by this thought.

It is what she always wanted.

And it is in the comfort of this thought that sleep takes her.